"What's this all about," asked the captain, his patience growing short.

"It's about destiny, Picard," answered the young bald man. "About a Reman outcast who—"

"You're not Reman," Picard reminded him.

That stopped the Praetor for a moment. "And I'm not quite human," he said. "So what am I? My life is meaningless as long as you're alive. What am I while you exist? A shadow? An echo?"

Picard shook his head. "If your issues are with me, then deal with me. This has nothing to do with my ship and nothing to do with the Federation."

"Oh, but it does," countered Shinzon. "We will no longer bow like slaves before anyone. Not the Romulans and not your mighty Federation. We're a race bred for war.

"For conquest."

STAR TREK®
NEMESIS

A novelization for young readers by John Vornholt

Based on the story by John Logan & Rick Berman & Brent Spiner

and the screenplay by John Logan

Based on Star Trek® created by Gene Roddenberry

ALADDIN PAPERBACKS

New York London Toronto Sydney Singapore

First Aladdin Paperbacks edition December 2002

™, ®, & © 2002 Paramount Pictures. All Rights Reserved.

This book is published by Aladdin Paperbacks,
an imprint of Simon & Schuster, Inc.,
under exclusive license from Paramount Pictures.

ALADDIN PAPERBACKS
An imprint of Simon & Schuster
Children's Publishing Division
1230 Avenue of the Americas
New York, NY 10020

Designed by Sammy Yuen Jr.
The text of this book was set in font Times.

Printed in the United States of America
2 4 6 8 10 9 7 5 3 1

Library of Congress Control Number 2002113930

ISBN 0-689-85627-X

For Michael the Blademaster

STAR TREK® NEMESIS

CHAPTER 1

Praetor Hiren tried not to roll his eyes as he listened to the same debate he had been hearing for weeks. Voices echoed in the vast chamber of the senate, but Hiren's gaze drifted out the cantilevered windows at the golden-hued sky. Dusk was settling over the imperial spires and towers of Romulus. It was the end of a day and the end of an era— an era when scheming and guile had ruled the empire. Now only brute force was recognized, making the Romulans little better than Klingons.

The Praetor sneered at the two commanders standing before him. They were so full of themselves, so certain of their warbirds and their weapons. *Did they fight in the wars of colonization? Did they battle people too proud to be crushed, such as humans and Vulcans?* Force was not enough with these capable enemies; only the proven ways of diplomacy, espionage, and sabotage worked to keep them off-balance. Yet here was another military master with a great fleet, ready to claim power by sheer force . . . and sheer waste.

The droning voice rose in volume, and Preator Hiren was forced to look back at the hawk-faced commander, who bellowed and shook his fist at the senators gathered in the great chamber. "What you do not seem to understand is this is a chance to make ourselves stronger than ever before! I beg you not to let prejudice or *politics* interfere with this alliance!"

Alliance? thought Hiren snidely. *This is more like the servants taking over the house.*

The second commander waved his hands, trying to placate the disgruntled politicians. "Praetor . . . senators," he began, taking a softer tone. "What my colleague is saying is that Shinzon represents an *opportunity* for the empire. If handled properly, he and his people can heighten our own glory."

"It's already too late to go back," insisted his comrade. "We must move forward *together*! And when his forces join ours, not even the Federation will be able to stand in our way."

Praetor Hiren waved his hand, unable to stand any

more of this prattle. "Enough!" he snapped. "The decision has been made!"

He glared at the two commanders. "The military does not dictate policy on Romulus. The senate has considered Shinzon's proposal and rejected it. He and his followers will be met with all deliberate force and sent back to that black rock they came from. Do I make myself clear?"

"Praetor," said the younger commander, bowing and backing away. The other said nothing, but his eyes held contempt as he bowed.

"The subcommittee on military affairs will be meeting tomorrow to prepare our tactical response," added Praetor Hiren. "You will attend."

"Yes, sir." Turning smartly on their heels, the two commanders strode toward the massive doors at the end of the senate chamber. The tension seemed to leave the room as well, and a degree of dignity was restored.

The Praetor sighed and turned to the colleague beside him. "Now, Senator," he said, "you were speaking of a trade affiliation with Celes II?"

"Yes, Praetor," he answered with a nod. "The trade committee has concluded that an agreement is in the best interests of the Empire. We recommend dispatching a diplomatic mission to open negotiations."

Hiren heard a grunt to his right, and he turned to see a

female senator scowling at him. "Senator Tal'Aura, you disagree with the motion?" he asked.

The regal Romulan shook her head. "No, sir. I would say 'negotiation' is to be advised. I support all diplomatic overtures . . ." Her voice trailed off, and she looked thoughtful. "But if you will excuse me, Praetor, I have an appointment with the Tholian ambassador."

Praetor Hiren nodded, knowing that Tal'Aura was one of those who attempted to be neutral on the issue of Shinzon. No matter. He didn't need her vote anyway. Tal'Aura stood and walked briskly out the door, leaving a small silver box on her desk. *Perhaps it is her jewelry box.* A buzz of conversation continued in the chamber, and the Praetor turned to the remaining senators.

"Then I will call for a vote on the motion to open trade negotiations with Celes II," announced Hiren imperiously.

Movement caught his eye, and he turned to look at the silver box. It had twitched. Another senator also peered at the gleaming object as the top sprung open. Slowly it began to unfold like a bizarre metallic flower. A beautiful halo of energy hovered above the box and twisted into a double-helix pattern. Suddenly a bright green beam filled the entire chamber.

Just as suddenly, the delicate light show ended, and the

Praetor grumbled. "Would someone please tell me what that was?"

When the senators just shrugged, Hiren turned to a centurion and said, "Alert security"—he noticed a potted plant behind him begin to shrivel—"and have them run a—"

The words choked in the Praetor's mouth, and a burning sensation swept over him. He tried to stand, but he had lost all feeling in his legs. All around him, the senators squirmed and panicked in their seats, but it was too late. A scream died in the Praetor's throat as the flesh melted from his bones. In his last moment of life, he saw the silver box vanish in the ripple of a transporter beam.

Earth

Captain Picard took a breath of clean Alaskan air and let his gaze travel from the crystalline sky to the majestic mountain range. He could smell the spruce and pine, as well as the sweeter scents of the flower arrangements. A more perfect place on Earth—or anywhere in the galaxy— he could not imagine. As Will Riker's ancestral home, it was a fitting spot to end one journey and begin another.

His eyes swept across the familiar faces arrayed before him at the long, gayly decorated table. They were his family, although none of them was related by blood. These people had shared danger, triumph, and failure with him.

He knew that any of them would give his or her life for him, and he for them. But giving life was not necessary today—only giving joy.

They awaited his words, as they so often had. Despite his pleasure, the captain tried to maintain a measure of dignity, as befitted his stiff white uniform.

"Duty," began Picard. "A starship captain's life is filled with solemn duty. I have commanded men in battle. I have negotiated peace treaties between implacable enemies. I have represented the Federation in first contact with twenty-seven alien species. But none of this compares to my solemn duty as . . . best man."

Laughter greeted his remarks, and no one looked happier than the bride, Deanna Troi. Will Riker beamed at his new wife, and Picard marveled at how their love had endured. On again, off again, spanning the years and other loves—at last they were united as they were always meant to be. Now it seemed inevitable, just as it was inevitable that Will would leave the *Enterprise.*

With a sigh, the captain said, "Now, I know that on an occasion such as this it is expected that I be gracious and fulsome with praise on the wonders of this blessed union. But have you two considered what you're doing to me? Of course *you're* happy, but what about *my* needs? This is all an inconvenience—"

The captain paused for more laughter, which he waved off. "While you're happily settling in on the *Titan,* I'll have to train my new first officer. You all know him. He's a steely sort of fellow who knows every word of every paragraph of every regulation by heart. A stern martinet who will never . . . ever . . . allow me to go on away missions."

Picard motioned to the android at his side, and Data nodded. "That is the regulation, sir. Starfleet Code section twelve, paragraph four—"

"Data," warned Picard in a mock-serious tone.

"Sir?" asked the android innocently.

"Be quiet." More laughter cascaded across the great table. The captain sighed with annoyance. "Then there's the matter of my new counselor. No doubt they'll assign me some soft-spoken, willowy thing who'll probe into my darkest psyche as she nods her head and coos sympathetically. Isn't that right, Deanna?"

Deanna nodded her head and cooed sympathetically, and her friends laughed. Picard's gaze traveled along the table to a vibrant red-haired woman, whose wedding he had attended a lifetime ago. He had also been best man on that occasion.

"I notice Dr. Crusher laughing along with the rest of you," said Picard. "As most of you know, the doctor will also soon be leaving the *Enterprise* to assume command of

Starfleet Medical. Again I'm forced to ask, Beverly, have you considered what you're doing to *me*? I'll probably get some old battle-ax of a doctor who'll tell me to eat my vegetables and put me on report if I don't show up for my physical on time."

"It'll serve you right," she replied.

Captain Picard looked serious for a moment as he returned his attention to Will and Deanna. "Really, it's not too late to reconsider—" Their joyous smiles told him that they had no regrets—not on this glorious day.

"No?" asked Picard with resignation. He lifted his glass for a toast and allowed himself a very wide grin. "Will Riker, you have been my trusted right arm for fifteen years. You have helped keep my course true and steady. Deanna Troi, you have been my conscience and guide. You have helped me to recognize the best parts of myself . . . you are my family."

With pride, he concluded, "And in proper maritime tradition, I wish you clear horizons. My friends, make it so." Captain Picard finished his toast, and everyone at the great table raised a glass and drank merrily.

Later that night, after the wedding party had moved to a beautiful pavilion which overlooked the mountains, Captain Picard mingled among the guests. A jazz band played a sprightly tune, and many were dancing. Others sat at their tables, quietly conversing. Despite the joy of the occasion, Picard couldn't help but to feel a little nostalgic, because this was the end of an era. There was no other way to look at it.

Beverly Crusher stepped to his side and gave him an amused look. "Sort of like losing a son and gaining an empath, isn't it?" she asked.

"You're being a big help," replied the captain thoughtfully.

"If you start tearing up," said the doctor, "I promise to beam you out. Level one medical emergency."

He gave her a smile which admitted that his emotions were a bit torn. In truth, Beverly, Deanna, and Will were long overdue to leave his command and move on to challenges of their own. He should be grateful that he could keep Data, Geordi, Worf, and the rest of his senior staff a little longer. Of course, their replacements would be more than capable; they would be the best Starfleet had to offer.

"Mom! Captain!" called a voice, breaking him out of his reverie. He and Beverly turned to see a handsome young man in a lieutenant's uniform striding toward them. Here was one officer who had left his command a bit too early, but no one could deny that Wesley Crusher had been the brightest of the lot.

"Hello, Wesley," said Picard warmly. "It's good to see you back in uniform."

"Suits him, doesn't it?" agreed his mother proudly.

The young man gave them a sheepish smile, and Picard asked, "Are you looking forward to serving on the *Titan*?"

"Very much," Wes answered eagerly. "I have the night duty shift in engineering. We have a double-refracting warp core matrix with twin inter-mix chambers that—"

His attention drifted as a pretty girl passed by. She graced him with a smile, and he began to inch after her. "Oh, excuse me," said Wes. "See you later, Mom."

Beverly shrugged and gave Picard a smile. "All he's seen and done in the last few years . . . it must be a relief to get back to normal."

"Normal," repeated Picard thoughtfully. He didn't say that it was hardly a normal day when he lost half his senior staff. Oh well, the *Titan* would certainly enter the fleet with one of the most experienced crews ever assembled. Then he would again feel like a proud parent.

Alyssa Ogawa approached Beverly and engaged her in a medical question, and Picard let his attention drift to the table behind him, where Geordi La Forge and Guinan were seated.

"I still can't believe he finally popped the question," said La Forge, shaking his head.

Guinan tilted her gigantic mauve hat and gave him a smile. "What makes you so sure *he* popped the question?"

"Counselor Troi?" asked Geordi in alarm. "You gotta be kidding."

"You have to keep an eye on us quiet, soulful types," replied the enigmatic El-Aurian.

The engineer leaned forward and asked, "You ever think about getting married again?"

She shrugged. "Maybe. But like I always say, why buy the Denubian seacow when you can get the milk for free?"

Worf moved slowly toward the table, and Picard could tell that he was still suffering a bit from Riker's bachelor party. He plopped down beside Geordi and massaged his skull ridges.

"Romulan ale should be illegal," declared the Klingon.

"It is," answered Geordi with amusement.

"Then it should be more illegal." Worf groaned and gently rested his head on the table.

Captain Picard felt a tug on his arm and turned back to Beverly. With a smile, she led him toward the bride and groom, who were making their rounds. Both Will and Deanna were beaming as they approached the captain, and he felt certain in his heart that their marriage would endure. They had waited a long time for this— they had waited until they were certain.

"It was a lovely toast," said the radiant bride.

"It was from the heart," answered Picard.

Deanna touched his arm. "And you needn't worry. I'll brief your new counselor on everything she needs to know."

"Don't you dare," answered Picard with a smile. "You already know too much about me. Now, you promised there are no speeches during the ceremony on Betazed."

"No, no speeches," Riker assured him. He suppressed a grin. "No clothes either."

Before the captain could question that bit of etiquette, the band stopped playing, and Data's voice carried across the pavilion.

"Ladies and Gentlemen and invited transgendered species," began the android, "in my study of Terran and Betazoid conjugal rites, I have discovered it is traditional to present the happy couple with a gift. Given Commander Riker's affection for archaic musical forms, I have elected to present the following as my gift in honor of their conjugation."

Data lifted his chin and without a moment's hesitation began to sing in a clear ringing voice. After a moment, the band began to follow him, recognizing the old Terran song, "Blue Skies."

The band picked up the tempo as Data began to sing the familiar chorus.

The entire crowd was smiling and swaying along to the music, except for one. Worf lifted his head off the table and groaned loudly.

"Ugghhh . . . Irving Berlin," grumbled the Klingon. His head thumped back to the table.

Will Riker fidgeted on his feet; he looked as if he wanted to join the band.

"All right, go ahead," said Deanna, giving him her blessing.

Will eagerly rushed toward the bandstand and grabbed a spare trombone. Once he joined the musical accompaniment to Data's singing, the song really began to jump. The captain held his hand out to the deserted bride.

"May I have this dance?" he asked Deanna.

"With pleasure, Captain." The Betazoid gracefully took his hand.

From the corner of his eye, Picard saw Beverly turn around and find Worf, seated alone. "Commander," she asked, "do Klingons swing?"

"I am unwell," he answered.

"Don't worry. I'm a doctor." She pulled him onto the dance floor and made a space beside the captain and the counselor.

"I'm so glad you made it back to the *Enterprise* before I left," said Beverly to the big Klingon.

"I was not suited for the life of a . . . diplomat," he answered.

"Who'd have guessed?" replied the doctor.

Both the counselor and captain laughed as they swept across the dance floor. Listening to Data sing while Will played trombone and the entire crew reveled into the night—it was perfect. *Not only is this a celebration for Will and Deanna,* thought the captain, *it's a reward for the entire crew and fifteen years' worth of tense moments and dire situations.* Like the happy couple, they had survived every conflict together and had emerged intact, full of love and respect for each other.

Picard brushed a crisp white sleeve at the corner of his eye, dabbing away a tear. Then he let the music fill his heart as he whirled the joyful bride across the dance floor.

Hours later Captain Picard stood in his quarters aboard the *Enterprise* and surveyed his small but impressive collection of wine bottles. His guest was not a wine connoisseur, but this was still a rare day: the introduction of a new first officer. Only one vintage would do for that. He took a bottle of red from the rack and held it up to the light.

"For a special occasion," he announced with pride, "Chateau Picard."

Using a corkscrew that was also well-aged, the captain carefully uncorked the treasured vintage. "They say a vintner's history is in every glass—the soil he came from, his past, his hopes for the future."

He poured two glasses and delivered one to his guest, who was seated on the couch. "So . . . to the future," he toasted, lifting his glass.

"To the future." His new first officer looked at him curiously, waiting to see what the captain would do with his glass of red wine.

Picard took a sip, letting the tart fruity liquid play across his tastebuds. He swished the wine in his mouth, spreading the delicate flavor, then he finally swallowed. Data did exactly the same thing in the same order, ending with an identical smile of satisfaction.

"Sir," said the android, "I noticed an interesting confluence of emotion at the wedding. I could not help wondering about the human capacity for expressing both pleasure and sadness simultaneously."

The captain sat beside his colleague and studied the color of the wine in his glass. "Certain human rituals—

weddings, birthdays, funerals—evoke strong and very complex emotions, because they mark important transitions in our lives."

"They denote the passage of time," observed Data.

"Not just the passage of time, but the presence of time within us," answered Picard. "They make us aware of our mortality. These occasions encourage us to think about what's behind and what lies ahead."

The android nodded thoughtfully. "And you were particularly aware of this feeling of transition, because Commander Riker will be leaving to assume command of the *Titan*?"

"Will and Deanna leaving the *Enterprise*," added Picard glumly. "Beverly going to Starfleet Medical—"

"And this makes you *sad*?"

The captain took a thoughtful sip of wine. "Well . . . I suppose it does a bit. I'm very happy for them, of course, but I'm going to miss them. The ship will seem . . . incomplete without them."

"That is because you are used to their presence," said Data. "Their proximity brings you comfort."

"Yes," agreed Picard, "and, frankly, I almost envy them as well. They've made important choices. They're going to have great challenges ahead of them. New . . . new worlds."

The captain took another sip of wine and looked at his

Ressikan flute lying on the coffee table. That was a memento from another life, which he had been blessed to experience in the blink of an eye. At the time it had been frightening and confusing, but the years had let him appreciate the unique gift from the Kataan probe. Often he thought he had been granted more lives than Data's cat, and the flute was proof of that. Despite all of his experiences, there were still many courses he had not steered.

Picard lowered his glass and said, "Seeing Will and Deanna today made me think about some of the decisions I've made. Devoting myself to Starfleet . . . not marrying or having children—all the choices that led me here."

Data frowned slightly, digesting his words. "The choices I made have led me here as well," he remarked. "This is the only home I have ever known. I cannot foresee a reason for leaving."

"You never know what's over the horizon, Data," said the captain with a knowing smile. "Before too long you'll be offered a command of your own."

The android peered at him, as if he had never really considered such a thing. "If I were . . . I believe my memory engrams would sense the absence of your proximity. I would . . . 'miss you.'"

"And I you," agreed the captain with a warm smile. "Now, you make a toast."

Looking very solemn, the android raised his glass and said, "To . . . new worlds."

"New worlds," echoed Picard as the two old comrades toasted the future.

CHAPTER 2

Romulus

Footsteps echoed in the dimly lit corridor outside the chamber of the Romulan Senate, and torches flickered along the walls. Commander Donatra was possibly the most beautiful ship's captain in the Romulan fleet, and she never hesitated to use that beauty when it was necessary. She wondered whether this meeting would be such an instance.

Beside her strode Commander Suran, a grizzled veteran of a dozen wars and one of the most respected leaders in the fleet. He didn't look happy.

"The fleet commanders are nervous," complained Suran. "They've agreed to remain at their given coordinates and await his orders. But they're anxious to know what's going on here."

"I don't blame them," answered Donatra bluntly. "We can't keep them in the dark forever."

"But in darkness there is strength," hissed a third voice coming from the shadows.

Donatra nearly jumped out of her boots, but she kept a calm look on her face as she waited for the newcomer to join them. From a shadowy alcove a cadaverous figure slunk toward them. His ashen face and sunken cheeks made him appear like a specter of the undead. Compared to their ornate uniforms, the Viceroy of Remus wore simple robes, unbefitting his rank.

Without another word, the Reman led them into the Senate Chamber. The first thing Donatra saw was the Romulan crest, an imposing bird-of-prey holding a planet in each claw. The great crest dominated an entire wall, and beneath it stood a young officer who looked even more out of place in this chamber than the Remans. It was hard to believe that the biggest fleet in the Romulan Star Empire was controlled by this creature:

A human.

The shaven-headed youth motioned to the Romulan crest. "Consider it," he said. "The great symbol of the empire. But the bird-of-prey holds two planets, Romulus *and* Remus, their destinies conjoined."

He brushed his austere Reman uniform, then went on,

"Yet for generations one of those planets has been without a voice. We will be silent no longer."

There were perhaps ten people in the great chamber, most of them Reman, but it still seemed eerily deserted. One of the few Romulans was Senator Tal'Aura, the one who had engineered the emptying of this chamber. Five fearsome Reman guards eyed the Romulans suspiciously, but Shinzon was his usual charming self.

"Join us, commanders," said the human. "Now, what's the disposition of the fleet?"

"They're holding position," answered Suran.

"And?" demanded the leader.

The old commander bowed. "They will obey, Praetor."

The leader nodded with satisfaction. "It's imperative we retain their allegiance, or our great mission will be strangled before it can truly draw breath."

"They support your intentions, sir," said Donatra carefully. "But they require evidence of your . . . shall we say . . . sincerity."

He regarded the commander coldly, but his face finally broke into a smile. "And they'll have it."

He walked toward a three-dimensional holographic star chart on the far wall and motioned to the Neutral Zone. Like a great stain, it stretched between the Romulan Star Empire and Federation space. "Tell the fleet that the days of negotiation and diplomacy are over. The *mighty* Federation will fall before us, as I promised you. The time we have dreamed of is at hand. The time . . . of *conquest*."

With purpose, the new Praetor stepped into the region of the chart designated with the Federation symbol. His fist swept through the familiar logo as he said, "Cut off the dragon's head, and it cannot strike back."

With that, he paused in thought, and Donatra wondered what was troubling the young man. *Perhaps Shinzon is reconsidering.*

"And how many warbirds will you need to 'slay the dragon'?" she asked.

He looked at her innocently. "You don't approve of my oratory."

"Pretty words are of little use in battle," answered Donatra.

"Wars are fought and civilizations made and lost over pretty words like 'glory' and 'honor' and 'freedom,'" said Shinzon. "You miss so much of life, Commander, looking only at battle maps and fleet protocols—"

She started to protest his remark, then Shinzon added, "In any event, I will need no warbirds."

Both Donatra and Suran stared at the cocky human, wondering if he had gone crazy.

"Praetor," said Suran evenly, "you have the *whole fleet* at your disposal. They supported the coup. They'll follow you."

He turned his back to them to study the chart. "The *Scimitar* will serve my needs."

"But surely—"

"I came this far alone." Shinzon turned to his Reman warriors and corrected himself. "*We* came this far alone. We require no assistance from the fleet. Now leave me."

With sullen expressions, Commander Suran and Senator Tal'Aura strode toward the door, but Donatra lingered for a moment. She saw Shinzon turn to his Viceroy.

"Are we prepared?" asked the human.

"Yes, Praetor." The cadaverous figure bowed.

Walking slowly, Donatra reached the doorway just as Shinzon said, "So many years for this moment. . . . Bring him to me." The Reman warriors bowed low to their master.

The *Enterprise* sliced through space at low warp enroute to Betazed for the second wedding ceremony and reception. All hands were on the bridge, fully recovered from the festivities on Earth. Worf finally looked fit, Captain Picard noted, but the big Klingon still didn't seem any happier.

Several crewmembers were gathered at Worf's tactical station. "I won't do it," he told them.

"It's *tradition,* Worf," insisted Counselor Troi. "You of all people should appreciate that."

The Klingon struggled for words. "A warrior does not appear without his clothing. It leaves him . . . vulnerable."

Commander Riker suppressed a smile. "I don't think we're going to see much combat on Betazed."

"Don't be too sure," cautioned Deanna. "Mother will be there."

That brought a deeper scowl to the Klingon's face, and he again declared, "I won't do it."

"Won't do what, Mister Worf?" asked Picard innocently as he joined them.

"Captain," said Worf with a great heave of his chest, "I think it is inappropriate for a Starfleet officer to appear . . . *naked.*"

"Come now. A big, strapping fellow like you?" said the captain cheerfully. "What are you afraid of?"

Deanna laughed out loud, and Worf turned back to his console. His forehead ridges furrowed as something caught his attention. "I'm picking up an unusual electromagnetic signature from the Kolarin system."

"What sort of signature?" asked Picard.

Worf glanced at Data before he answered. "Positronic."

That is *unusual,* thought the captain, because Data's neural net was the only known source of positronic emissions.

Geordi La Forge, Picard, Riker, and Data gathered

around the engineering substation, where La Forge was homing in on the source of the readings. "It's very faint," said the engineer, "but I've isolated it to the third planet in the Kolarin system."

"What do we know about the planet?" asked the captain.

"Uncharted," said La Forge. "We'll have to get closer for a more detailed scan."

The captain turned to Data and asked, "Theories?"

The android cocked his head thoughtfully. "Since positronic signatures have only been known to emanate from androids such as myself, it is logical to theorize that there is an android such as myself on Kolarus Three."

"How many of you did Dr. Soong make?" asked Geordi.

"I thought only myself and my brother, Lore," replied Data.

Riker pointed to the star chart on Geordi's screen. "Diverting to the Kolarin system takes us awfully close to the Romulan Neutral Zone."

"Still well on our side," added Picard as he studied the same chart. This wasn't an urgent matter, but Picard could see the curiosity in Data's yellow eyes as he stared at the readings. Any possibility of finding another being like himself was bound to intrigue him.

"I think it's worth a look," concluded the captain. "Don't worry, Number One, we'll get you to Betazed with time to spare."

"Thank you, sir," said Riker with relief. He glanced nervously at his new bride.

Picard looked at Worf and said, "Where we will *all* honor the Betazoid traditions." The Klingon scowled but said nothing.

Riker strode down to the helm and gave the order. "Mister Branson, set course for the Kolarin system. Warp five." Deanna shot him a glare, and he corrected himself. "Warp seven."

After a moment, Branson reported, "Plotted and laid in, sir."

"Engage," ordered Riker.

Geordi La Forge looked up to see his best friend staring at him. "What do you think, Data?" he asked. "A long-lost relative?"

The android didn't respond, but it was clear that his positronic brain was considering the possibilities. Could there be another of Dr. Soong's wondrous creations?

A day later the *Enterprise* was in orbit around the uncharted planet known as Kolarus III. The Class-M planet was in a region of space ravaged by ghostly ion storms, which made taking sensor readings more difficult. Captain Picard was conscious of every second this investigation was taking from their journey to Betazed. He hovered over La Forge's station on the bridge, hoping the latest modification to sensors had worked.

"I read six distinct positronic signatures," La Forge finally reported, "spread out over a few kilometers on the surface."

"What do we know about the population?" asked the captain.

"Isolated pockets of humanoids," answered Data from his station. "It appears to be a prewarp civilization at an early stage of industrial development."

Geordi narrowed his new ocular implants at his readouts. "Captain, I don't recommend transporting. That ion storm doesn't look very neighborly. It could head this way without much warning."

"Understood," said the captain with a nod. He motioned and said, "Data, Worf, you're with me."

The human, android, and Klingon walked toward the turbolift, where Commander Riker cut them off. He held up his hand as he had so many times before in a futile attempt to keep the captain from danger. "Captain, I hope I don't have to remind you—"

"I appreciate your concern, Number One," said Picard, "but I've been itching to try out the *Argo*."

Riker broke into a grin. "I'll bet."

"Captain's prerogative, Will," said Picard warmly. "There's no foreseeable danger . . . and your wife would never forgive me if anything happened to you."

Worf, Data, and Picard stepped into the turbolift. As the doors shut, the captain added, "You have the bridge, Mister Troi."

The look on Riker's face was priceless, as was the laughter from the bridge crew.

The turbolift whisked them to the shuttlebay, where they boarded the *Argo,* Starfleet's newest version of short-range personnel transport. Larger than a regular shuttlecraft, the *Argo* had a particularly large cargo bay in the stern. This allowed her to carry ground vehicles, several dozen passengers, or a good amount of emergency supplies. Despite her extra size, the *Argo* had a relatively small cockpit that allowed her to be flown by a crew of two.

For this mission, Captain Picard was mainly interested in the *Argo*'s sensors and transporters; they were more advanced than what a normal shuttlecraft possessed. With Data piloting the craft, they entered the atmosphere and found themselves cruising over a vast desert. There were rugged canyons and mountains, not unlike parts of Arizona that Picard had visited, although the sparse vegetation made Kolarus III look more like Death Valley in California.

After landing, Picard, Worf, and Data boarded an all-terrain vehicle, which was also new to the captain. Of course, he insisted upon driving, and they roared out of the cargo doors at perhaps too great a speed. In a cloud of dust, the ATV screeched to a stop, and Data used the dashboard control panel to shut the cargo doors of the *Argo*. The ship was now protected, although there didn't appear to be anyone around who could bother it. In the backseat of the ATV, Worf quickly fastened his seatbelt.

Data checked his tricorder and reported. "The closest signature is two kilometers to the west . . . that direction, sir." The android pointed toward the craggy horizon, which shimmered in the heat waves of the desert floor.

"Thank you, Data." Picard tightened his grip on the steering wheel. "Let's see what she can do!"

The ATV roared off in a cloud of dust, with Picard enjoying his stint behind the wheel. *Imagine, at one time in Earth's history, such a mode of travel was common,* he thought. Beside him Data clung to the door, and Worf braced himself against the rollbar with both arms. It was a little bouncy, but nothing they couldn't take, decided the captain.

Above the roar of the engine and churning sand, Data said, "I will always be baffled by the human predilection for piloting vehicles at unsafe velocities."

Picard smiled and gave the vehicle more juice, and they rumbled across the desert. Data checked his tricorder again, then pointed to the left. "Over that rise, sir . . . half a kilometer."

The ATV rolled on until Data signaled for a stop. All three of them scanned the terrain as they stepped onto the sand, but there was nothing in this wasteland that bore any resemblance to Data.

"The radiant EM field is interfering with my tricorder," said the android, "but we are within a few meters of the signal."

Picard knelt down and poked in the crusty desert, where only a bit of lichen grew. Suddenly he heard Worf growl, and he turned to see the Klingon trying to shake a disembodied arm off his ankle. The hand had Worf's ankle in a tight grip, but he reached down and brutally yanked it off. Grimacing, he held the arm aloft as the hand continued to writhe like something from a nightmare.

Data moved closer with his tricorder and reported. "It appears to be . . . a robotic arm."

"Very astute," muttered Worf.

"Why is it moving?" asked Picard.

Data cocked his head. "Like me, it has been designed with modular power sources."

30

"Mister Worf, if you please." The captain motioned to the ATV, and Worf stowed the robotic arm in the rear cargo trunk.

"The next signature is one kilometer to the south," said Data.

After several bumpy rides, they found a leg, the torso, the second leg, second arm, and all the pieces of an android identical to Data. The only thing missing was the head, and now Data had a bearing on that. Several of these pieces were still moving, and Worf looked uneasily at the disassembled android writhing in the trunk.

"The final signature is approximately one hundred meters to the north, sir," reported Data.

They drove on until they found what looked like Data's head, lying in the dust like an old rock. Having no appendages, it wasn't moving.

"It's . . . you," said Worf in amazement.

The android nodded in agreement. "The resemblance is . . . striking."

They climbed out of the vehicle and slowly approached the eerie object. Data leaned down for a closer look, and the eyes in the head suddenly popped open. The partial Data looked at his twin with childlike wonder.

"Why am I looking at me?" asked the head in a voice that sounded like Data's.

"You are not looking at yourself," answered Data. "You are looking at me."

The eyes in the android head moved toward Worf. "You do not look like me."

"No," agreed the Klingon.

Data leaned down. "I would like to pick you up now. May I do that?"

The head was now looking at Picard. "You have a pretty shirt," it said.

"Thank you," replied the captain.

Data gently picked up the head, and Picard watched the strange spectacle of two identical faces gazing at each other.

"Fascinating," remarked Data.

Without warning, a boulder behind them exploded, showering them with gravel. The three visitors spun around to see a tribe of ragged natives racing toward them in primitive vehicles. Nevertheless, they had plasma weapons, which they didn't hesitate to use.

"Come on!" barked Picard, waving his comrades toward the ATV.

CHAPTER 3

"Shall we try some unsafe velocities?" snapped Picard. He gunned the engine as more plasma explosions erupted around them. Everyone had jumped into the all-terrain vehicle, with Data still gripping the head that looked like his own. The captain floored the energy pedal, and they roared across the desert floor, away from the tribesmen who were chasing them. As dust flew, the three visitors bounced along the desert plain of Kolarus III.

Worf manned the phaser canon in the back of the ATV, shooting beams at the pursuing vehicles. The explosions weren't close enough to kill, but several of the cars crashed into the craters he made. Still a dozen vehicles ripped through the smoke and dust, right on their tail.

Although Data was holding the android head, it

couldn't take its eyes off Picard. "You have a shiny head," it remarked.

Data frowned and said, "This is not an appropriate time for a conversation."

"Why?" asked the head innocently.

"Because the captain has to concentrate on piloting the vehicle," answered Data, his voice barely audible over the squealing tires.

"Why?" asked the head.

"Data!" snapped Picard, wanting him to concentrate on their escape.

"Sorry, sir." The android lowered the inquisitive head and looked at his control panel.

Picard followed their original tracks as best he could, but there was too much dust from spinning tires and plasma blasts to see much. He knew their pursuers were close behind, because he could hear the roar of their engines. They seemed to be spreading out to avoid Worf's phaser blasts. Even with his daring driving and superior equipment, their foe had the numbers.

With Data giving directions, they finally spotted the *Argo* on the shimmering horizon. Then Picard gasped. It was surrounded by more of the belligerent locals. "Mister Data!" he called.

The android worked the dashboard console, and the

Argo lifted off the ground under his control. The natives near the craft rushed for their vehicles and weapons, and many of them spotted the ATV. Now the visitors were trapped between two hostile forces. It was chaos as their vehicle weaved between plasma blasts coming from both directions.

Data flew the *Argo* ahead of them, but there wasn't enough time to land the craft and pick them up. The angry locals were closing in from both sides when Picard spotted a rise in the terrain.

"Data!" he called, pointing to the crest. From the dashboard of the ATV, the android piloted the *Argo* over the rise, where it disappeared. There wasn't time to think too much about this maneuver, which was a good thing. Picard spun the steering wheel and veered sharply toward the crest as Data opened the *Argo*'s rear cargo doors. A plasma blast to their left nearly knocked them out of their seats.

As they roared up the incline, Picard realized at the last moment that the rise was actually a cliff. There was nothing but a dead drop into a massive gorge. With no time to stop, the ATV flew off the ground into the air, with the abyss yawning beneath them. Data calmly positioned the *Argo* to match their trajectory, and they shot through the air into the open cargo doors. Behind them an army of hostile natives screeched to a stop at the edge of the cliff.

When they finally rolled to a halt in the cargo bay, Data

quickly closed the doors behind them. Picard climbed out on shaky legs, but he tried to look nonchalant as he wiped a bit of dirt off the windshield. He smiled at his stunned comrades and strode toward the *Argo*'s cockpit. Data looked at Worf, who let out a relieved gust of air.

Picard, Riker, Data, Dr. Crusher, and La Forge took the disassembled android to the main engineering lab on the *Enterprise*. They mounted it in a stasis frame, still unjoined but in a humanoid shape. While Geordi analyzed the torso, Beverly Crusher peered quizzically into the blank eyes of the android.

"I think you have nicer eyes," she told Data.

Picard leaned closer to hear what Data would say. The android replied, "Our eyes are identical, Doctor."

Beverly stepped back from the rig which held the various parts of Data's twin. The captain figured that Data, La Forge, and the doctor could put him together in short order. Perhaps they should defer to Data, who would appear to be a close relative of this android.

Commander Riker looked to his chief engineer, who was busy studying the android's torso. "Geordi?"

La Forge looked up from his tricorder. "Well, he seems to have the same internal mechanics as Data, but not as much positronic development. The neural pathways aren't nearly as sophisticated. I'd say he's . . . a prototype. Something Dr. Soong created before Data."

"Do you have a name, sir?" Data asked the head, which was stationary at eye level.

"I am the B-4," answered the head.

"Be-fore," said Picard thoughtfully. "Dr. Soong's penchant for whimsical names seems to have no end."

"Can you tell me how you came to be on the planet where we found you?" asked Data.

The B-4 replied simply, "I do not know."

"Do you remember anything of your life before you were on the planet?" asked Data.

"No," answered the B-4. His attention switched to Will Riker. "You have a fuzzy face."

The captain sighed, thinking that they might never learn any more than this. "Keep me informed, Number One," he said. "And please, put him back together."

Data peered at the B-4 and asked, "Do you know who I am?"

"You are me," said the head.

"No," Data corrected him gently. "My name is Data. . . . I am your brother."

The lights were suitably dim in the crew lounge for the late hour, and few of the tables were occupied. Still Deanna

Troi was always happy to be in the company of these two males, her new husband and an old boyfriend, Worf. Any differences between Will and Worf had been long forgotten. Their fifteen years aboard the *Enterprise* had seemed like several lifetimes rolled into one, and it was exciting to think there was another lifetime ahead of them.

Worf ate heartily as usual, and he nodded as he listened to Deanna's wedding plans. She liked the way ceremonies were being held on both worlds, with the wedding drawn out as long as possible. "And after the ceremony on Betazed," she told Worf, "we have three entire weeks for our honeymoon."

The Klingon shook his head, as if that seemed excessive.

Riker said, "We're going sailing on the Opal Sea. We've booked an old-fashioned solar catamaran. Just us and the sun and the waves."

"It seems a very . . . soft honeymoon," replied Worf. He wiped some food from his moustache.

"It's meant to be relaxing," countered Deanna.

Worf frowned gravely. "A Klingon honeymoon begins with the Kholamar desert march where the couple bonds in endurance trials. If they survive the challenge they move on to the Fire Caves of Fek'lhr to face the demons of Gre'thor."

"Well, that sounds relaxing too," said Riker with amusement.

"It's . . . invigorating," answered Worf, puffing out his chest. His attention was diverted, and Troi followed his eyes to the entrance of the lounge. Data entered, carefully leading the B-4 android.

"So they've got him up and running," said Riker in a low voice.

The Klingon scowled. "He's a very . . . unusual android."

"Runs in the family," said Riker, smiling at his own joke.

But Deanna Troi was not smiling. She watched Data lead his twin to an empty table and show him how to sit. The B-4 stared blankly into the distance, while Data instructed him how to use a napkin. Even with Data as a teacher, the B-4 was a poor learner. Their friend was such a bundle of curiosity and intelligence, while this immature copy was like a simple child. Troi didn't know which troubled her more: the dull face of the B-4 or Data's eagerness to teach him.

The *Enterprise* had set course for Betazed once more, and Captain Picard relaxed in his ready room. He thought about listening to some opera—Berlioz, perhaps. There was the mystery of Data's double, but that could turn out to have a logical explanation. None of their scans of Kolarus III had turned up any clues, and they may never know where the B-4 came from.

Picard glanced at the food replicator on the bulkhead, and he wondered if someone had tried to replicate Data. If so, they had failed, creating an incomplete copy instead. Data had always seemed like a unique being to his shipmates; he was one of a kind, just like any human.

How much should we do to make the B-4 more like Data? That was up to Data to decide.

The captain rose from his desk and went to the replicator. "Earl Grey, hot," he ordered. A moment later a cup of steaming tea appeared on the replicator pad. He picked it up just as a comm signal sounded.

"Captain," said the voice of Commander Riker, "you have an Alpha Priority communication from Starfleet Command."

"Acknowledged." The captain returned to his desk and activated his personal viewscreen. He was delighted to see the wry smile of Admiral Kathryn Janeway, who'd been captain of *Voyager* during her long odyssey across the Delta Quadrant.

"Admiral Janeway," he said. "Good to see you."

"Jean-Luc," she replied warmly. Janeway got right to

the point when she said, "How'd you like a trip to Romulus?"

Picard smiled warily. "With or without the rest of the fleet?"

"A diplomatic mission," answered the admiral. "We've been invited, believe it or not. Seems there's been some kind of internal political shakeup. The new Praetor, someone called Shinzon, has requested a Federation envoy."

Picard frowned. "New Praetor?"

"There's more," said the face on the viewscreen. "He's Reman."

Picard's surprised expression mirrored her own, and Janeway continued, "Believe me, we don't understand it either. You're the closest ship, so I want you to go and hear what he has to say. Get the lay of the land. If the Empire becomes unstable, it could mean trouble for the entire quadrant."

"Understood," answered Picard gravely.

Janeway glanced away and motioned to someone. "We're sending you all the intelligence we have, but it's not much. I don't need to tell you to watch your back, Jean-Luc."

"Not with the Romulans," he assured her.

Janeway smiled wryly and shook her red hair. "The Son'a, the Borg, the Romulans . . . you seem to get all the easy assignments."

"Just lucky, Admiral," said Picard with a sigh.

"Let's hope that luck holds. Janeway out." The blue laurel-wreath logo of the Federation blinked onto the screen, and Picard looked thoughtful as he rose to his feet. Of course the second wedding ceremony for Riker and Troi was now in serious danger of being postponed. He was glad they had at least managed the first ceremony, the one with clothing.

This mission was high priority, because a rupture in Romulan command was a serious matter. There were always elements who wanted to fight the Federation, and the Romulans had emerged from the Dominion War in better shape than most powers in the quadrant. Remans had usually operated in the background, although he was aware of Reman crews and troops. With any luck, they would understand the situation soon enough.

Captain Picard strode through the door of his ready room onto the bridge of the *Enterprise*. Everyone appeared relaxed, but that was about to change. Picard looked pointedly at the helm and ordered, "Lay in a new course. Take us to Romulus, warp eight."

Now everyone looked shocked, none more so than Will Riker.

"Aye, aye, sir," answered the helm officer, working his board. "Course plotted and laid in."

"Romulus?" asked Commander Riker with concern.

Picard nodded gravely. "I'm afraid the Opal Sea will have to wait, Number One." The captain went to his chair and pointed forward. "Engage."

After dropping down to impulse power to change course, the sleek starship cruised space for a moment before it elongated like a blue flame. Then it vanished into the darkness in a brilliant flash of tachyons, neutrinos, and plasma.

CHAPTER 4

Captain Picard sat stiffly in his chair in the observation lounge, gazing at the faces of his trusted comrades. Riker, Troi, Crusher, and La Forge all looked at Data as the android concluded his briefing. Data pointed to a videolog of the planets Romulus and Remus in orbit around the sun they shared. The image of Romulus was a familiar one, but Remus had always been the unknown half of the equation . . . until now.

"As you can see," Data went on, "one side of Remus always faces the sun. Due to the extreme temperatures on that half of their world, the Remans live on the dark side of the planet. Almost nothing is known about the Reman home-world, although intelligence scans have proven the existence of dilithium mining and heavy weapons construction. The

Remans themselves are considered an undesirable caste in the hierarchy of the Empire."

Riker cut in. "But they also have the reputation of being formidable warriors. In the Dominion War, Reman forces were used as assault troops in the most violent encounters."

"Cannon fodder," agreed Picard.

La Forge shook his head puzzledly. "Then how did a Reman get to be Praetor? I don't get it."

"We have to assume he had Romulan collaborators," answered Riker.

"A coup d'etat?" asked the captain.

Riker shrugged. "The Praetor's power has always been the Romulan fleet. They must be behind him."

Picard nodded in agreement, then turned to Data. "What have you learned about Shinzon?" he asked.

No images of the new Praetor flashed upon Data's screen. He answered simply, "Starfleet intelligence has only been able to provide a partial account of his military record. We can infer he is relatively young and a capable commander. He fought seventeen major engagements in the war, all successful. Beyond that, we know nothing."

The captain frowned at this lack of information. "Well, it seems we're truly sailing into the unknown. Keep at it. Anything you can give me would be appreciated. Dismissed."

Most of the officers filed out, but Commander Worf hung back to talk to the captain. "I recommend we raise shields and go to Red Alert, Captain," said the Klingon.

"Not quite yet, Commander," replied Picard.

"Permission to speak freely, sir," asked Worf. When Picard nodded, he went on. "I know the Romulans, and I don't trust them. They live only for conquest. They are a people *without* honor. We are alone, well inside their territory. I recommend extreme caution."

Picard respected the opinion of his tactical officer, but appearances were important. "For better or worse, we're here on a diplomatic mission. I have to proceed under Federation protocols. But at the first sign of trouble, you can be assured, those protocols will no longer apply."

"Thank you, sir," answered Worf with some relief.

Geordi La Forge frowned, squinting at Data with his ocular implants. His friend was joined to the B-4 android by cables to their neural ports. Connected head-to-head by these cables, the two androids looked more alike than ever. But the B-4 had a blank expression as it gazed around the engineering lab, which gave Geordi an eerie feeling. *The B-4 is like an empty tank getting filled with high-quality fuel,* Geordi thought.

"I can't believe the captain went along with a memory download," said La Forge, shaking his head.

Data answered, "Captain Picard agrees that the B-4 was probably designed with the same self-actualization parameters as myself. If my memory engrams are successfully integrated into his positronic matrix, he should have all my abilities."

"He'd have all your memories, too," said Geordi. "You feel comfortable with that?"

"I feel nothing, Geordi," answered the android simply. "It is my belief that with my memory engrams he will be able to function as a more complete individual."

La Forge frowned. "An individual more like you, you mean."

"Yes," answered Data honestly.

"Maybe he's not supposed to be like you," argued Geordi. "Maybe he's supposed to be just like he is."

"That might be so," allowed Data. "But I believe he should be given the opportunity to explore his potential."

Geordi checked his readings, then stepped back. "Okay . . . we're done." Carefully he removed the connecting cables and closed the panels in their heads.

Data turned to his twin and asked, "Do you know where you are?"

"I am in a room with lights," answered the B-4. He studied the lights as if they were important.

"Can you remember . . . our father?" asked Data.

"No," came the blunt reply, and Geordi looked at his friend with concern.

The android plunged onward. "Do you know the name of the captain of this vessel?"

"No," answered the B-4.

Geordi peered at him. "Do you know my name?"

"You have a soft voice," answered the B-4.

Data managed not to look disappointed, but Geordi knew he was.

"Data," he said gently, "he's assimilating a lot of programming. Remember, he's a prototype—a lot less sophisticated than you are. We just don't know if his matrix will be able to adapt or if he'll be able to retain anything. We should give him some time."

Data appeared to be studying some circuitry embedded in the B-4's neck. "What purpose does this serve?" he asked.

La Forge peered at the tiny coupler, which he had inspected before. "It seems to be a redundant memory port. Maybe it's for provisional memory storage in case his neural pathways overload."

"Dr. Soong must have found it unnecessary in later versions," concluded Data.

"It's possible the extra memory port is interfering with the engram processing," offered Geordi. "Mind if I keep him here and run some diagnostics?"

"No, I do not mind," answered the android as he looked somberly at the B-4.

"Don't give up hope, Data." Before his friend could reply, La Forge waved his hand. "I know, I know. . . . You're not capable of hope."

"I am not," said the android, still gazing at the B-4.

Data rose to leave, and the B-4 rose too, as if to follow him out. "No, remain with Commander La Forge," said Data. "He is going to try to make you well."

La Forge watched his friend leave, wondering what he was feeling. *It must be tough,* thought Geordi, *to be the only one of your kind.* With both the B-4 and his brother, Lore, Data thought he had found someone who was like him. But they never really were.

The blue-brown planet of Romulus, as seen from orbit, was eerily quiet, and it had been for a very long time. Captain Picard could swear he could hear the seconds ticking off his computer screen as he pressed the panel in his ready room.

"Captain's Log, Stardate 56844.9," he began. "The *Enterprise* has arrived at Romulus and is waiting at the designated coordinates. All our hails have gone unanswered. We've been waiting for seventeen hours."

There was nothing else to say, so he logged off and

returned to the bridge. His crew looked tense, and they were out of guesses about Romulan intentions. Worf was making cracking sounds with his neck, which seemed to be irritating Counselor Troi. She stood and paced by La Forge's engineering station.

Riker grumbled, "Why don't they answer our hails?"

"It's an old psychological strategy, Number One," answered Picard, "to put him in a position of dominance and make us uneasy."

"It's working," muttered Riker.

The captain turned to his empath. "Counselor?"

"They're out there, sir," answered Deanna Troi, staring at the quiet planet on the viewscreen.

Picard strode to her side and studied the darkness beyond the planet, where Remus was clearly visible in space. *Has the silent partner really taken over the business?*

Worf cut into his thoughts. "Sir, I recommend we raise shields."

"Not yet, Mister Worf," answered the captain evenly.

"Captain," said Riker, "with all due respect to diplomatic protocols, the Federation Council's not sitting out here. . . . *We* are."

"Patience," answered Picard. "Diplomacy is a very exacting occupation. We can wait."

"*Captain,*" warned Data.

Everyone turned to the viewscreen to see a magnificent Reman warbird materialized out of nowhere. The awesome vessel hovered in front of the *Enterprise,* bristling with visible weapon ports. Still it maintained the raptorlike lines of traditional Romulan design, and Picard marveled that such a large ship could be cloaked, as it obviously had been.

Riker rose from his seat.

"Raising shields," announced Worf.

"No," said Picard firmly.

"Captain—" the Klingon began to protest.

"Tactical analysis, Mister Worf," ordered the captain, wondering what all those weapons were.

"Fifty-two disruptor banks," reported Worf, "twenty-seven photon torpedo bays, primary and secondary phased shields."

"She's not out for a pleasure cruise," Riker quipped.

"She's a predator," agreed Picard. The Reman vessel looked as if it could never be used for anything but war.

"We're being hailed," said Worf.

"On screen." The captain took his station in front of the viewscreen.

The being that appeared on the screen was startling in his gaunt appearance, with a face like a hairless rodent.

Despite his stooped height, he was so pale that he looked like a wraith from some old horror story. *So this is a Reman,* thought Picard. He was a well-dressed one, too, and he looked as if he was used to command, probably from the shadows he preferred. Even now, the light on their bridge was unusually dim.

"*Enterprise,*" he intoned, "we are the Reman warbird *Scimitar.*"

"Praetor Shinzon," said Picard warmly, "I'm pleased to—"

"I am not Shinzon," snapped the Reman. "I am his Viceroy. We are sending transport coordinates." With that, the transmission abruptly ended, and the warbird *Scimitar* returned to the viewscreen.

"Not very chatty," grumbled Riker.

Picard let out a sigh; at least matters were progressing. He looked around and saw that the relief bridge crew was standing by. "Away team," ordered the captain, "transporter room four."

Riker, Troi, Worf, and Data followed him toward the turbolift, energized now that the endless wait was over. Minutes later they gathered in the transporter room and took their places on the platform. For now, this was just another diplomatic call, Picard tried to tell himself, giving the order to transport.

Picard and his team materialized inside an austere observation lounge on the *Scimitar*. There was no furniture and very little decoration, only a large rug made from crude materials. The only light seemed to be natural light coming through the etched dome, and there was very little of that.

A voice came from the shadows. "I hope you'll forgive the darkness. . . . We're not comfortable in the light."

"Praetor Shinzon?" asked Picard.

A figure stepped from the shadows into the dim light, and it was all they could do not to gasp. It wasn't that he was as eerie looking as the Viceroy; no, he was quite handsome, with a slim body and regal bearing. What was startling was that this creature was human.

As Shinzon stepped through a dim beam of light, his features looked even more human . . . and young. Picard judged him to be under thirty, with a face that was oddly familiar. He felt a pang of recognition he could not place, but the light was dim.

Shinzon gazed at the captain with just as much interest. *Surely the Praetor expected to meet humans,* thought the captain, *but that's not what we expected.* No one was able to muster any words until Shinzon himself spoke.

"Captain Picard," he began, "Jean-Luc Picard. I don't mean to stare, it's just—well, you can't imagine how long

I've been waiting for this moment. I always imagined you taller. Isn't that odd?"

Their host glanced at Data. "You may scan me without subterfuge, Commander Data."

Given permission, the android lifted his tricorder and began to scan Shinzon. At that moment, the Reman Viceroy slunk from the shadows.

"And you're not as we imagined you," Picard said, finding his voice.

"No?" asked Shinzon with amusement.

"You are human," said Worf.

"Commander," said the young man. Then he spoke in fluent Klingon, greeting Worf as a warrior and brother, if Picard's knowledge of Klingon was correct.

Tersely, Worf replied in Klingon that he would prefer a better brother. Pickard knew that even when Romulans looked like humans, Worf didn't like them.

Shinzon laughed at this affront, and Picard demanded, "Why have you asked for our presence here?"

But their host was now distracted by Deanna Troi, and he gazed frankly at her.

"Praetor?" asked Picard.

"I've never met a human woman," said Shinzon with reverence.

"I'm only half human," replied the Betazoid.

Shinzon never took his eyes off Deanna, even when her new husband moved closer. He motioned to her and said, "Deanna Troi of Betazed . . . empathic and telepathic abilities, ship's counselor. All of this I knew, but I didn't know you were so beautiful."

"You seem very familiar with our personnel," said Riker, crossing his brawny arms.

"I am, Commander Riker." Shinzon continued to stare at Deanna Troi, and he reached for her face. "May I touch your hair?"

Picard interrupted. "Praetor, we've come to Romulus on a matter we were assured was of great importance. If you have anything to say to us as representatives of the Federation, I suggest you do so now."

Shinzon kept his eyes upon Troi, and the captain wondered if this scrutiny bothered her. She seemed more interested in watching the Viceroy, who crept slowly toward them. Picard couldn't read the Reman's face, but his body language seemed protective of the young Praetor.

Shinzon didn't seem to remember the rest of them existed—only Counselor Troi. "On the world I come from, there's no light. No sun. Beauty isn't important. . . . I see now there's a world elsewhere."

"Praetor Shinzon," insisted Picard.

He turned to the captain, smiling apologetically. "Yes, I'm sorry, Captain. There's so much we have to talk about."

Picard's lips thinned, and he said, "I would be interested to know what we are talking about."

"Unity, Captain!" declared Shinzon. "Tearing down the walls between us to recognize we are one people. Federation and Romulan, Human and Vulcan, and Klingon and Reman. I'm speaking of the thing that makes us the same. We want peace."

Picard and his crew had nothing to add to that bold declaration. If the new Praetor was really serious, this could be the beginning of a golden age of peace.

Shinzon went on. "I want to end the centuries of mistrust. I want to be your ally, not your enemy. As a first step I propose we eliminate the Neutral Zone and begin a free and open exchange of goods and ideas."

Picard looked at him warily. "And the Senate supports you?"

"I have dissolved the Senate," replied Shinzon evenly. He waved his hand at his guests. "Right now you're thinking this all sounds too good to be true. And you're wondering why the *Scimitar* is so well armed. Is this the ship of a peacemaker . . . or a predator?"

Picard thought that the young man had read his mind fairly well, and he said nothing. So the Praetor continued.

"But you're also thinking the chance for peace is too promising to ignore. Above all, you're trying to decide if you can trust me. Am I right?"

"Yes," admitted Picard.

Shinzon nodded with satisfaction. "Then perhaps the time has come to add some illumination to our discussion. Computer, raise lighting four levels."

At once light beams shot from hidden lamps in the observation lounge, and the visitors were treated to normal illumination. For the first time the away team got a good look at their host, and Picard's breath caught. The rest of the away team looked from him to Shinzon and back.

That's me! he wanted to shout. It was like looking into a mirror fifty years ago.

Shinzon sensed his amazement and smiled warmly. "Allow me to tell you a story that I hope will clarify my position," said the young man. "When I was very young I was stricken with an odd disease. I developed a hypersensitivity to sound. The slightest whisper caused me agony."

The captain watched him carefully, wondering where this was going. "No one knew what to do," said Shinzon. "Finally I was taken to a doctor who had some experience with Terran illnesses, and I was finally diagnosed with Shalaft's syndrome. Do you know of it, Captain?"

Picard scowled in anger. "You know I do."

"Then you know it's a very rare syndrome," said Shinzon. "Genetic. All the male members of my family had it. Eventually I was treated. Now I can hear as well as you can, Captain."

He stepped closer to Picard, but the elder human did not back away. "I can see as well as you can," added Shinzon. "I can feel everything you feel. In fact, I feel exactly what you feel. Don't I, Jean-Luc?"

Picard could scarcely believe his eyes, his ears, or his heart. Because all of his senses told him he was staring at an immature version of himself. *How? Cloning? A freak of nature?* His mind whirled. What kind of human could grow up on the planet Remus and take over the Romulan Empire?

"Come to dinner on Romulus tomorrow," Shinzon told the captain. "Just the two of us. Or should I say . . . just the *one* of us."

The rest of the crew looked confused, and they were even more startled when Shinzon drew a knife and cut his own arm. He handed the blood-streaked blade to Data and calmly said, "I think you'll be wanting this. Tomorrow then, Captain. We have so much to discuss."

Barely controlling his emotions, the captain tapped his commbadge and said, "Picard to *Enterprise*. Five to beam out."

The away team vanished in five shimmering columns of light.

In sickbay Captain Picard looked on nervously as Dr. Crusher studied the blood-stained knife under a proton-microscope. Surrounded by readouts and computer analyses, it only took her a few seconds to reach a conclusion.

"There's no doubt, Captain," said Beverly. "Right down to your regressive strain of Shalaft's Syndrome . . . he's a clone."

Anger rose within him, and Picard said through clenched teeth, "When was he . . . created?"

"About twenty-five years ago," answered the doctor. "They probably used a hair follicle or skin cell."

"Why?" asked Riker, also sounding angry.

"Believe me, Number One. I'm going to find out," vowed Picard. "Contact Starfleet Command and inform them of the situation. I need to know where he came from." He motioned to his counselor and strode toward the door. "Deanna."

The Betazoid followed him out of sickbay and down the corridor. "I would say he's been trained to resist telepathy," she reported. "What I could sense of his emotions were erratic—very hard to follow."

"Is he sincere about wanting peace?" asked Picard. His anger ebbed slightly as he walked.

"I don't know," she answered. "The strongest sense I had was that he's very curious about you. He wants to know you."

"Does he now?" answered Picard with a scowl.

Deanna was quick to stop him. "Captain, your feelings are appropriate. The anger I sense in you is—"

He cut her off. "Can you imagine what it was like to stand there and look at him? To know an essential part of you had been *stolen*? I felt powerless . . . violated!"

"What you're feeling is a loss of self. We cherish our uniqueness, believing that there can only be one of us in the universe."

"And now there are two," muttered Picard.

Deanna shook her head. "No, Captain. Biology alone doesn't make us who we are."

Picard rubbed his chin thoughtfully as he considered her remarks. Shinzon was only a copy of him physically; in upbringing, education, and experience he was a different man entirely. For a human to rise from a lower caste and become Praetor of the Romulan Empire, he had to be driven, a born leader. No doubt, Shinzon also had to be ruthless.

After leaving Captain Picard in the corridor near sickbay, Deanna Troi went to the cabin she now shared with Will. It was convenient sharing quarters, but she still wished she were alone with Will on their honeymoon. They would have been floating on the Opal Sea by now, if only the Romulans hadn't changed rulers. Somehow it all seemed like a practical joke designed to mess up her wedding. But there was nothing funny about the Praetor's ship and the odd silence of the Romulans.

Fear had seized this solar system, and she could feel it.

In their quarters, Will was hard at work on a handheld padd, with more padds scattered about his table. Deanna sat at her desk and updated the crew records, getting all her case histories ready to turn over to the new counselor. She was leaving everyone on the *Enterprise* in more or less good condition, although she sometimes worried about how hard they worked. For example, her husband looked as if he were both tired and frustrated.

She rose from her desk and walked over to him. "Will, you need to rest."

When he ignored her, Deanna's tone grew stern. "As ship's counselor, I'm recommending you get some sleep."

Will set the padd on the table and wearily rubbed his eyes. She began to massage the tense muscles of his neck, and he finally started to relax. He looked up at her with tired eyes. "Some honeymoon."

She kissed him gently on the temple and stroked his hair. "We have time."

He touched her hand as she massaged his temples. "Imzadi—"

Her hands continued to curl through his dark locks of hair, but his hair began to change color before her eyes. It became a shock of blond hair, then blond stubble, closely shaved. When she tried to pull away, he grabbed her hands and held them in place, and his face looked up at her with a smug smile. It wasn't Will—it was Shinzon!

"Imzadi," he said, gripping her hands tightly.

"No!" shouted Deanna. She wanted to run, but it felt as if her legs were rooted to the deck. "This isn't real!"

"Can you feel my hands? Are they real?" asked Shinzon.

As he looked up at her, his face turned into the ghastly visage of the Viceroy. Now Deanna was completely frozen in terror, and a scream strangled in her throat. Shinzon's voice seemed to be coming from the pale, blue-veined lips of the Reman.

"I'm with you, Imzadi," he rasped. "I'll always be with you now."

"No!" Mustering all her willpower, Deanna finally managed to push him away.

He jumped up in alarm and stared at her. "Deanna?"

asked Will with concern. Now it was Will again . . . her beloved Will. She stared at him, disbelieving, until her emotions were certain that the waking nightmare was over. Then she sunk in to her husband's arms and clung to his broad shoulders.

She couldn't tell him . . . but the Praetor and Viceroy had been inside her mind.

CHAPTER 5

Commander Donatra sat stiffly in the main chamber of the Romulan Senate, noting the heavy curtain which had been installed over the observation windows. Now the room was like a well-furnished but abandoned cave. Her compatriot, Commander Suran, was pacing angrily in front of the new Praetor. The beautiful Senator Tal'Aura squirmed uncomfortably in her seat. They all knew this meeting was not going well.

Commander Suran stopped pacing for a moment and turned to Shinzon as the Viceroy retreated further into the shadows. "I don't understand the reason for the delay!" snapped Suran.

"You don't have to understand," replied Shinzon evenly.

"And bringing the *Enterprise* here?" muttered Suran.

"What possible purpose could that serve?"

"I have a purpose," Shinzon assured him.

"Then perhaps you will enlighten us," snapped the veteran commander.

"Silence, *Romulan*!" growled Shinzon. Anger flared on the handsome face, but he quickly controlled it. "You must learn *patience,* Commander. Do you know where I learned it? In the dilithium mines of Remus. Spend eighteen hours every day under the lash of a Romulan guard and you'll soon understand patience."

Suran gulped and bowed his head as he backed away. "Praetor."

"Now go," ordered Shinzon, dismissing them. "I have some personal business."

The senator and the commanders moved briskly toward the door, but the Praetor motioned after them. "Commander Donatra, please remain," he ordered.

Hmmm, thought the Romulan. Perhaps this was her opportunity. She returned his gaze with her dark eyes and moved toward him. She had never admitted it to anyone, but she found young humans to be very attractive, especially ones who wielded power so easily.

She stepped closer to him, feeling his tension and desire. Had he ever given any time to romance? She doubted it.

He spoke. "We talked about the power of words once. Do you remember?"

"Yes, Praetor," she answered.

His gaze penetrated her eyes. "Here's a word I would like you to consider: 'allegiance.' It's something I demand from those who serve me."

"Do I serve you?" she asked suggestively.

He nodded. "Yes . . . and, I think, faithfully. Commander Suran, on the other hand, gives me pause."

As he moved closer, she was certain that he would fall under her seductive skills. "Here is another word, Praetor," said Donatra. " 'Trust.' Do you trust me? How far does that trust extend? How deep does it go?"

She circled him, whispering in his ear. "What must a commander do to prove herself faithful to you?" She stroked his smooth, unlined cheek. "What must a woman do?"

Roughly, he grabbed her hand and jerked it away. "You're not a woman," he said with contempt. "You're a *Romulan.*"

Donatra nearly spit in his face, but she curbed her instincts. Still the commander glared at him as she backed away.

"Now we know each other, Commander," said Shinzon. "Serve me faithfully, and you will be rewarded. And keep those lovely eyes on Commander Suran. At the first sign of treachery—"

She nodded her head. "Dispose of him."

"Then you will have proven yourself. Now go," ordered the Praetor.

Bowing her head, Donatra moved toward the door. But Shinzon motioned one more time. "And Commander," he said, "if you ever touch me again, I'll kill you."

At the door, she turned to peer back into the dim light, and she saw the Viceroy approach Shinzon. The Reman did something odd: he put his hand on Shinzon's chest and leaned very close to the human. Then a Reman guard held the door open for Donatra, forcing her to leave.

In the corridor she stopped to think about what she had seen. It was strange, but the Viceroy had almost looked like a doctor examining his patient.

Alone in Data's cabin, the B-4 android stared blankly at the bulkhead. Suddenly a signal activated his hidden programming, and the B-4 jumped to his feet. He raced to Data's computer console, sat down, and began to work. His fingers moved with such velocity over the controls that they were no more than a blur. Gradually the ship's systems yielded to his mastery.

In a vast, mostly empty senate chamber, Captain Picard sat in a quiet corner, having dinner with the new Praetor. They dined on Terran food with a tasty Romulan ale. Still Picard didn't have much appetite, and he poked at his food. His younger counterpart ate with gusto, just as Picard had at the age of twenty-five. Perhaps it was their conversation which took away his appetite.

"And when I was ready, they were going to replace you with me," Shinzon explained with delight. "Put a Romulan agent at the heart of Starfleet. It was a bold plan."

"What happened?" asked Picard.

"As happens so frequently here on Romulus," said Shinzon with contempt, "a new government came to power. They decided to abandon the plan. They were afraid I'd be discovered and it would lead to war."

When Picard refilled his glass with ale, Shinzon cringed. "Romulan ale," he muttered. "I'm surprised—I can't stand it."

"You'll acquire a taste for it," said Picard with amusement. He didn't add that it had taken him many diplomatic dinners to appreciate Romulan ale. He looked again at the younger version of himself; it was difficult not to stare.

Now Shinzon smiled. "It's not quite the face you remember."

"Not quite," said the captain.

The Praetor shrugged. "A lifetime of violence will do

that. My nose was broken, and my jaw . . . but so much is the same. The eyes, you recognize the eyes."

"Yes."

"Our eyes reflect our lives, don't they?" asked Shinzon. "Yours are so confident."

They both reached for a carafe of water at the same time, and both withdrew their hands. "After you, Praetor," said Picard.

"Age before rank, Jean-Luc," answered the younger man with a smile.

Picard poured water for both of them. "So I'm not as tall as you expected?"

"I always hoped I would hit two meters," answered Shinzon.

"With a full head of hair," added Picard.

"There is that."

After a moment, the captain asked, "How did you end up on Remus?"

"They sent me there to die," answered Shinzon. "Imagine a stark planet with towering mountains . . . and hellish winds. The winds blow all the time because of convection currents from the lighted side of the planet. Our only crops grow in the twilight areas between the two sides of Remus."

The young man shrugged. "Then again, I spent most of my youth underground—in the dilithium mines. The mineshafts go so deep into the planet that some of them pass through magma. There are flames everywhere . . . and laborers who never see the light."

He shook his head. "How could a mere human survive the dilithium mines? I was only a child when they took me . . . I didn't see the sun or the stars again for nearly ten years. The only thing the Romulan guards hated more than the Remans was me."

Picard could almost envision the young child, dressed in rags, digging dilithium many kilometers beneath the surface of a hostile world. It was not the kind of place that would have bred a kind, compassionate human being.

"But one man took pity on me," said Shinzon, "the man who became my Viceroy. He taught me how to survive."

Picard could imagine the cadaverous Reman protecting the young boy. Even today, he always hovered nearby, waiting to guide his charge through danger. *Where is he right now, I wonder?*

Shinzon went on. "And in that dark place, where there was nothing of myself, I found my Reman brothers. They showed me the only kindness I ever knew."

He turned to gaze at the Romulan crest on the wall. "For

thousands of years," said Shinzon, "the Romulan Senate has met in this chamber and dictated the fate of its sister planet. But the time has come for us to live as equals."

"You're doing this to liberate the Remans?" asked Picard.

"No race should be a slave to another," answered the Praetor. "That was the single thought behind everything I've done—building the *Scimitar* at a secret base, assembling my army, finally coming to Romulus in force. I knew they wouldn't give us our freedom. We would have to take it."

"And how many Romulans died for your freedom?" asked Picard bluntly.

"Too many," said Shinzon with a sweep of his hand. "But the point is, the Empire is finally recognizing there's a better way. And that way is peace."

Picard said nothing, because he didn't want to doubt such a noble sentiment. But was it more than a sentiment?

"You don't trust me," said Shinzon.

"I have no reason to," answered the captain.

His host insisted, "You have every reason, if you had lived my life and experienced the suffering of my people . . . you'd be sitting where I am."

"And if you had lived my life, you would understand my responsibility to the Federation. I can't let personal feelings unduly influence my decisions."

"All I have is my personal feelings," said Shinzon. The young man seemed to be wrestling with a thought he couldn't put into words. "I want to know . . . what it is to be human. You're the only link I have to that part of my life. The Remans gave me a future. You will tell me about my past—"

"If I can," said Picard carefully.

"Were we Picards always warriors?" asked Shinzon.

"I'm not a warrior, Shinzon. Is that what you think?"

"I don't know," admitted the young man.

Picard cocked his head and said, "I think of myself as an explorer."

"Then were we always explorers?"

"No," answered the captain. "I was the first Picard to leave our solar system. It caused quite a stir in the family. But I had spent my youth—"

"Looking up at the stars," said Shinzon, finishing his sentence.

"Yes."

"And you dreamed about what was up there. About—"

"New worlds," said Picard. He peered curiously at his young clone. "Shinzon, I'm trying to believe you."

"I know." The Praetor met his intense gaze.

Picard went on. "If there's one ideal the Federation holds most dear it's that all men, all races, can be united. From the first time the Vulcans came to Earth we've sought a future of peace. Nothing would make me more proud than to take your hand in friendship . . . in time, when trust has been earned."

"In time, Jean-Luc," agreed the Praetor.

After Captain Picard had returned to his own ship, Shinzon sat in the empty senate chambers, thinking about their conversation. *A farmer*—the Picards had been farmers, tilling the land. He didn't want to hear that; *it made him more freakish than he already was.* Shinzon heard the soft padding of his Viceroy's footsteps behind him.

"He's more gentle than I thought," said the human. "And he has a sense of humor."

"This was a mistake," answered the Viceroy sternly. "We're wasting time."

"*My* time," Shinzon reminded his underling. "I'll spend it how I choose."

They looked tensely at each other for a moment, then the Viceroy remarked, "Don't forget our mission, Shinzon. We should act. Now."

The Praetor rose to his feet and adjusted his sash. Perhaps the time for pleasantries was over.

"We'll return to the *Scimitar,*" said Shinzon. "Prepare yourself for the bonding."

• · • · •

As soon as Captain Picard stepped from the turbolift onto the bridge of the *Enterprise,* he could tell something was wrong. Both La Forge and Data were studying readouts on the engineering console, and Worf was working his tactical station.

"Sir!" barked the Klingon. "We've had an unauthorized access into the main computer."

"Source?" asked the captain.

Worf looked at La Forge, who shook his head. "It's going to take some time to find out. The data stream was rerouted through substations all over the ship."

Picard clenched his teeth. "What programs were accessed?"

The engineer shook his head. "That's what I don't get. It's mostly basic stellar cartography—star charts, communications protocols, some uplinks from colony tracking stations. It's not even restricted material."

Picard turned back to Worf and said, "Set up a security program to detect any unusual data stream rerouting. If it happens again, we want to be ready."

The Klingon nodded and went to work. Geordi's voice broke in once again. "There's something else," he said, pointing to his readouts. "I was reviewing the sensor logs. When the *Scimitar* decloaked, there was a momentary spike in the tertiary EM band. You're not going to believe this but . . . it's thalaron."

Picard felt a lump in his throat, and he tried to gulp it down. "Let's get an opinion from Dr. Crusher."

The captain stood in a sickbay laboratory with Crusher, La Forge, and Data. All around them, viewscreens showed graphic illustrations of Thalaron research. Beverly Crusher turned her attention from one screen to another, making notes on her padd.

"I thought thalaron radiation was theoretical," said Picard, still in shock.

"Which is why our initial scans didn't pick it up," answered La Forge. "But he's got it, Captain."

"As I remember," said Picard, "thalaron research was banned in the Federation because of its *biogenic* properties."

Dr. Crusher nodded gravely. "It has the ability to consume organic material at the subatomic level. I can't overestimate the danger of Thalaron radiation, Jean-Luc. A microscopic amount could kill every living thing on this ship in a matter of seconds."

"Understood," said the captain. "Keep on it. I need to know what he has and how to neutralize any threat. Give me options."

The captain wandered into the corridor, thinking of these worrisome developments as he saw Data pull Geordi aside for a conference. *If the* Scimitar *had some kind of deadly new weapon, it might explain how Shinzon had achieved power over the Romulans,* Picard thought. And now someone had broken into their main computer. The two events might not be connected, but he suspected they were.

Still troubled, Captain Picard retired to his quarters. He tried to compose a report, but it was difficult to face his conflicting emotions. Just when he was beginning to like Shinzon, something happened to make him distrust the arrogant ruler. After a while, the captain found himself looking at the old photos of himself on his desk.

The old images showed a serious cadet, full of himself, certain of his future successes. In a youthful fight with Nausicaans, he had received a serious injury to his heart. He had survived, and his quick recovery had made him feel invincible. But Picard didn't feel invincible anymore. So it was oddly comforting to know there was a younger version of himself, like a son he had never met. Still, he couldn't really trust Shinzon, and Picard felt like a father who hated his own offspring.

A chirp sounded, signaling someone at his door. "Come!" he called. When the door opened and Beverly Crusher entered, he greeted her warmly. "Beverly, come in."

"You're working late," she said with mild disapproval.

She noted the pictures of young Jean-Luc on his desk.

"Remember him?" asked Picard.

Beverly smiled. "He was a bit cocky, as I recall."

"He was a fool," said the captain with a scowl. "Selfish and ambitious. Very much in need of seasoning."

"He turned out all right," remarked Beverly.

The captain crossed to his small viewport, which allowed him a partial view of the *Scimitar* in the distance. "I so wanted to believe Shinzon," he explained. "But the thalaron radiation can't be explained away. Whatever he's after, it's not peace."

"Is he very much like you were?" asked the doctor.

"Yes," answered Picard grimly.

A comm signal broke him out of his reverie. "Data to Captain Picard."

"Go on."

"Geordi and I have identified the source of the un-authorized computer access," the android reported. "And I believe we have also discovered an opportunity to gain a tactical advantage. We are in engineering."

"On my way," answered Picard.

Before he could reach the door, Beverly held out a hand to stop him. "Jean-Luc, I've known you for over thirty years. I watched you hold Wesley the day he was born. I watched you take your first command."

She glanced at his old photographs. "Whoever you were then, right now you're the man you've made yourself. Shinzon is someone else."

The captain sighed. "Yes, Doctor, I want to believe that." He strode out the door.

In a kind of trance, the Viceroy knelt before a candle flame burning in a small, dark room. Shinzon knelt across from him, feeling the Reman's great power as he joined his mind with Deanna Troi's.

"Imzadi," he said softly, knowing he was reaching the exotic creature on the *Enterprise*. She was making his head swim in a way he had never felt before. "Your heart doesn't constrain itself to mere logic. Your heart longs to discover me, to know me—"

He could see her in his head, and he went on. "You want to leave all of this behind and be with me. I can feel your hunger to know the Reman ways . . . the old ways." He was visiting her in her dreams. She struggled against him, but he could still control her. "I can feel your desire, Deanna—"

But she was not without mental power herself, and the room began to spin. The mental connection was fading, and Shinzon tried to hold the dark-haired beauty in his mind. But she was torn away from him.

The Viceroy slumped forward, almost touching the

candle flame. He resumed his composure and said, "The bond is broken."

"Find her again," ordered Shinzon.

Before the Reman could respond, an officer interrupted on the comm channel. "Praetor, we've received the transponder signal."

"On my way," announced Shinzon. He strode toward the curtained doorway, but a feeling of pain and weakness gripped him. Shinzon began to fall, but the strong arms of the Viceroy held him up.

The Reman put his hand on the Praetor's chest, and the pain and dizziness began to fade. Still it was a struggle to maintain his regal bearing. The Viceroy looked at him with an expression that was more grim than ever.

"It's accelerating," he said. "You have no more time for games."

"Have the doctors prepare," said Shinzon weakly. "I am going to the bridge."

With an effort, the Praetor made his way through the massive ship to the bridge. He lifted his chin and put on a brave act as he greeted his Reman crewmembers and engineers. "Comrades, begin the recovery."

The chief engineer nodded and worked the transporter console. In the center of the bridge, the B-4 android materialized in a flurry of sparkling ions.

"Welcome home," said Shinzon. He pointed to the engineers. "Begin the download."

As they worked, the Praetor went to the replicator and ordered an odd Terran beverage he had recently discovered: "Tea, hot."

Commander Riker looked with concern at his new bride as she lay on an examination table in sickbay. Dr. Crusher had scanned Deanna thoroughly and was now consulting her readouts. Captain Picard hovered on the other side of her bed, looking just as concerned. Neither man had ever seen Deanna quite so upset.

Beverly told her patient, "Aside from slightly elevated adrenaline and serotonin levels, you're completely normal."

"Can you describe it, Deanna?" asked the captain gently.

She gazed at him with tears of rage and fear in her eyes. "It was . . . a violation." Riker took her hand and held it helplessly.

With difficulty, Deanna went on. "Shinzon's Viceroy seems to have the ability to reach into my thoughts. I've become a liability. . . . I request to be relieved of my duties."

"Permission denied," answered Picard. "If you can

possibly endure any more of these . . . assaults . . . I need you at my side. Now more than ever—"

Before the words were out of his mouth, the captain began to dematerialize in the haze of a transporter beam. Riker hit his commbadge and ordered, "Worf! Raise Shields!"

But it was too late—Captain Picard was gone.

"They have cloaked," said Worf's angry voice. "The *Scimitar* is off our sensors."

CHAPTER 6

Captain Picard paced angrily across his cell in the brig of the *Scimitar*. That's where he assumed he was; it bore all the austere trappings of a Reman cell. More ghoulish was the medical apparatus visible just beyond the force-field guarding his door. Reman technicians silently prepared for what looked like a complex medical procedure. A metal chair was the focus of their attention, and it looked as if it could hold a man against his will.

Shinzon entered with the B-4 android following him. Captain Picard tried to calm himself, because there was always hope against an arrogant enemy like Shinzon. The captain noticed something odd on the clone's face: a spider-web pattern of tiny blue veins. He had never seen such veins on his own face.

"Hello, Jean-Luc," said the Praetor warmly.

"Why am I here?" demanded Picard.

"I was lonely," answered Shinzon. He noticed Picard staring at him, and he touched the veins on his face. "Perhaps I'm not aging as well as you did."

The Praetor motioned to his technicians, and one of the Remans approached the cell with a hypospray in his hand. The force-field vanished, and he stepped inside.

"What are you doing?" asked the captain, backing away.

"I need a sample of your blood," explained Shinzon amiably. "What do your Borg friends say? 'Resistance is futile.'"

Picard allowed the sample to be taken; he wanted a better opportunity than this to make a fight. As the technician worked, the captain glanced at the B-4 android, who stared blankly ahead.

Shinzon noticed his attention and said, "Yes, I learned there might be an existing prototype from a Cardassian historian. Then I went to a great deal of trouble to find it and scatter it about on Kolarus III. I knew it would pique your curiosity—a lure to make the *Enterprise* the closest ship to Romulus when I contacted Starfleet. The bait you couldn't refuse."

The Reman technician left the cell, and the force-field

was reactivated. The doctor went to the mysterious medical apparatus and analyzed Picard's blood sample.

The captain shook his head in amazement. "All of this so you could capture me?"

"Don't be so vain," snapped Shinzon. "After we found it, we made a few modifications. An extra memory port, a hidden transponder. I've now gained access to Starfleet's communications protocols. I now know the location of your entire fleet."

He turned to the B-4 and ordered, "You may go."

"Where?" asked the android.

"Out of my sight." The B-4 nodded obediently and left the brig.

Shinzon smiled. "It has more abilities than you might imagine. I've been training it to do little tasks for me, like your robot does."

"What's this all about?" asked the captain, his patience growing short.

"It's about destiny, Picard," answered the young bald man. "About a Reman outcast who—"

"You're not Reman," Picard reminded him.

That stopped the Praetor for a moment. "And I'm not quite human," he said. "So what am I? My life is meaningless as long as you're alive. What am I while you exist? A shadow? An *echo*?"

Picard shook his head. "If your issues are with me, then deal with *me*. This has nothing to do with my ship and nothing to do with the Federation."

"Oh, but it does," countered Shinzon. "We will no longer bow like slaves before anyone. Not the Romulans and not your mighty Federation. We're a race bred for war. For conquest."

Picard's lips thinned. "Are you ready to plunge the entire quadrant into war to satisfy your own personal demons?"

Shinzon scoffed, "It amazes me how little you know yourself."

"I'm incapable of such an act," declared the captain.

"*You are me!*" shouted Shinzon. "The same noble Picard blood runs in our veins. Had you lived my life, you'd be doing *exactly* as I." He moved closer and stared into Picard's face. "Look in the mirror and see yourself."

Picard shook his head, saying nothing. So the Praetor went on. "Consider that, Captain. I can think of no greater torment for you."

"It's a mirror for you as well," said Picard evenly.

Shinzon turned back to him and stared at his elder with a mixture of fear and admiration. He pointed to the bizarre medical apparatus. "Not for long, Captain. I'm afraid you won't survive to witness the victory of the echo over the voice."

• • · • •

On the bridge of the *Enterprise,* Worf tensed at his tactical station, anxious to do something against those who had stolen his captain. "No response to our hails," he reported to his shipmates yet again.

Geordi slammed a fist on his engineering station. "His cloak is perfect—no tachyon emissions, no residual antiprotons."

"Keep at it, Geordi," ordered Commander Riker. "Find a way in." The first officer rose from his command chair and stared at the stars on the viewscreen.

Worf growled, "Sir, we have to do something!"

The turbolift door opened, and Dr. Crusher strode onto the bridge, carrying a medical padd. She motioned to Riker. "Will, I need to talk to you."

Tired of pacing, Captain Picard stood wearily in his cell in the *Scimitar*'s brig. A feral-looking Reman guard watched his every move. When the outer door opened and the B-4 android entered, both Picard and the guard looked at him.

"Praetor Shinzon wants the prisoner on the bridge," said the B-4.

The Reman guard studied the Praetor's toy for a moment, then he turned to deactivate the force-field. The guard had begun to place arm restraints on the captain when the B-4 stepped forward and gave the Reman a

Vulcan nerve pinch. The guard collapsed onto the deck of the brig, and Picard bounded from his cell.

"My mission was a success, sir," said the android, now acting like himself. Picard realized Geordi and Data must have discovered how the B-4 had accessed their ship's systems, and they acted quickly to find his hidden transponder and place it on Data. Now Data was free to roam the *Scimitar*, acting as the B-4, who was held on the *Enterprise*.

"I have discovered the source of the Thalaron radiation. This entire ship is, essentially, a Thalaron generator. The power relays lead to an activation matrix on the bridge."

"It's a weapon?" asked Picard in astonishment.

Data nodded. "It would appear so."

"And the download?"

"He believes he has our communications protocols," explained Data. "But they will give him inaccurate locations for all Starfleet vessels."

"Good work," said Picard.

Data rotated his left hand and pressed a panel on his wrist, exposing a hidden compartment. He removed a small, silver disc and handed it to the captain.

"Geordi supplied me with the prototype for the emergency transport unit," he explained. "I recommend you use it to return to the *Enterprise*."

STAR TREK

"It'll only work for one of us," replied Picard.

"Yes, sir."

The captain shook his head. "We'll find a way off together."

He inserted the ETU back into Data's wrist, then he grabbed the guard's disruptor rifle and handed the weapon to his comrade. Picard took the smaller hand disruptor for himself and hid it under his tunic. Now it was time to find their way out of there.

With his disruptor rifle pointed at Picard's back, Data led the captain through the corridors of the *Scimitar*. To all they passed, he was the B-4 taking the prisoner to their master. Picard wore the Reman restraints loosely, ready to cast them off at a moment's notice. A group of Remans looked at the prisoner with undisguised loathing.

"Move, puny human animal," ordered Data, prodding the captain with his weapon.

Picard whispered, "A bit less florid, Commander."

Suddenly Shinzon, his Viceroy, and a Reman doctor crossed their path in an intersecting corridor. Picard and Data ducked into a shadowy doorway and waited until they passed out of sight. *They're probably on their way to the brig,* thought the captain, *where they will find a surprise.*

Picard and Data picked up their pace, moving through the unfamiliar ship until the alarm kiaxons sounded an

The *Enterprise* crew celebrates the wedding of Commander Riker (Jonathan Frakes) and Counselor Troi (Marina Sirtis). *(above)*

The best man (Patrick Stewart) and the matron of honor (Gates McFadden) share in the newlyweds' joy. *(right)*

Worf (Michael Dorn) discovers the source of
the positronic readings—an android arm.

La Forge (LeVar Burton) tries to unravel
the enigma of the B-4.

The crew is shocked to discover that the new Praetor
is neither a Romulan nor a Reman, but a clone
of Jean-Luc Picard, named Shinzon (Tom Hardy).

After meeting Shinzon, the captain wonders if
he is truly different from the ruthless Praetor.

Troi is confronted by Shinzon.

Shaken, the counselor asks to be relieved of her duties.

The Viceroy (Ron Perlman) has an advantage over
his adversaries in the darkened Jefferies tube.

Shinzon resolves to kill Picard.

For the first time in his career, Data (Brent Spiner)
disobeys a direct order.

alert. Harsh Reman commands blasted over the shipwide comm system.

"This way, sir!" said Data, steering him down another dimly lit passageway. "There is a shuttlebay ninety-four meters from our current location."

They sprinted through the twisting corridors, darting this way and that. Suddenly they heard footsteps ahead of them, and a cadre of Reman warriors cut them off. Picard tossed off his restraints and drew his handheld disruptor, while Data took aim with his rifle. The dark corridor was suddenly lit with sizzling disruptor beams and jarring explosions. Smoke began to blur the strobelike bursts of fire, and Picard and Data retreated in another direction.

Blindly the captain followed Data, knowing that if anyone knew the way through the chaos, it would be Data. They arrived at the shuttlebay door, which was reinforced and locked. Data tried the lock, but it wouldn't open.

"It seems to have an encrypted security system," he reported.

Disruptor beams streaked over their heads, and Data handed Picard his rifle. The captain returned fire while Data worked on the locks.

Firing with both hands, the captain shouted, "Alacrity would be appreciated, Commander!"

Data worked swiftly, his fingers a blur as they punched

numbers into the security panel. He said, "They are trying to override the access codes. Reman is really a most complex language with pictographs representing certain verb roots and—"

"While I find that fascinating, Data," said Picard, panting, "we really need that door open!" He laid down some blistering cover fire then slumped back against the bulkhead.

Suddenly the shuttlebay door slid open, and they ducked inside. As soon as the door slammed shut behind them, Picard blasted the mechanism with his disruptor, trying to disable it. Catching his breath, the captain turned to see a collection of small shuttlecraft, which looked more like fighter craft. There was a prominent disruptor turret on each tiny vessel.

Data peered at the craft. "According to the ship's manifest, they are Scorpion-class attack fliers."

Picard didn't care what they were as he jumped into the pilot's seat of the nearest craft. He could hear Reman warriors blasting at the shuttlebay door, trying to stop their escape. With a glance over his shoulder, Data climbed into the gunner's position at the rear.

After giving the controls a brief look, Picard pressed the keypad and powered up the Scorpion. He touched a small lever. "What do you imagine this is?"

"Port thrusters, sir," answered Data. "Would you like me to drive?"

Picard glanced back at the android with a look of disbelief. Nobody was going to drive but him, and he boldly began pressing buttons. Without warning, the Scorpion lifted off the deck, hovered for a moment, then began to move. Picard steered it toward the large external doors of the shuttlebay, but they remained stubbornly closed.

"Can you open the shuttlebay doors?" he asked his co-pilot.

"Affirmative, sir," answered Data as he worked his console. When nothing happened, he shook his head. "Negative, sir. They have instigated security overrides and erected a force-field around the external portals."

Picard shrugged. "Well then . . . only one way to go." He piloted the small craft around the shuttlebay until it faced the interior doors, where the Remans were trying to blast through.

Data frowned. "Do you think this is a wise course of action?"

"We're about to find out," answered the captain. "Power up disruptors and fire on my mark."

"Ready, Captain," answered the android, working his board.

"Fire!" barked Picard.

The Scorpion's disruptors blasted the doors into silvery slivers, sending Remans scrambling for cover. The small craft roared out of the shuttlebay into the corridor, banking sharply. It bounced against the bulkhead, sending off sparks and scraping noises. Startled Remans dove out of the way as the Scorpion zoomed down the corridor.

Spacecraft weren't meant to be flown inside other spacecraft, and it was all the captain could do to keep from smashing the craft to pieces. This was the most insane joyride he had ever taken, but it kept them ahead of the disruptor blasts. Data pointed out a direction to take, and Picard followed his navigator's advice.

A second later they roared through wide double-doors into the observation lounge, where they had first met Shinzon. Picard pulled back on the helm, and they shot upward toward the beautifully etched dome. Data fired disruptors, pulverizing the dome an instant before they flew through it and into space.

Aboard the *Enterprise,* the bridge crew was startled by the sight of a small shuttlecraft blasting from a cloak of shimmering space. It darted away from the warbird and streaked straight toward them. With a point in space to fix on, the *Enterprise* sensors zoomed in on the *Scimitar*. On sensors, Riker could see the *Scimitar* powering up a tractor beam, and he shouted, "Worf! Lock on transporters!"

A tractor beam shot across space from the *Scimitar*, stopping the tiny shuttlecraft dead, but they were an instant too late. "I have them, sir!" shouted Worf in triumph.

Picard's voice came over the comm channel. "Number One, emergency warp!"

The helm officer reacted instantly, and the *Enterprise* banked into a great arc and disappeared in a blazing halo of light.

Aboard the *Scimitar,* Shinzon stared with disgust at the empty stretch of space where his prey had made their escape. He slammed his fist on the arm of his command chair just as the weathered face of Commander Suran appeared on his viewscreen.

"This has gone far enough!" declared the veteran warrior.

Shinzon took a calming breath. "I thought we discussed patience, Commander."

"And mine is wearing thin!" said Suran through clenched teeth. "We supported you because you promised *action.* And yet you delay—"

Shinzon rose from his chair and straightened his tunic. The discolored veins in his face were more prominent than ever. "The *Enterprise* is immaterial," he said.

"They won't make it back to Federation space. And in two days the Federation will be crippled beyond repair. Does that satisfy you?"

The veteran commander still looked grim. "For the moment."

Shinzon narrowed his eyes at the Romulan. "When I return, you and I shall have a little talk about showing *proper respect*!" The Praetor made a motion to cut off transmission before the sniveling Romulan could complain any more.

At the great table in the senate chamber, several Romulans watched the image of Praetor Shinzon blink off the viewscreen. They sat in silence for a moment—an angry moment for Commander Suran, a fearful one for Senator Tal'Aura, and a reflective one for Commander Donatra.

"Does anyone in this room harbor any illusions about what he means by 'showing proper respect'?" asked Donatra.

Senator Tal'Aura cringed. "What's happening to his face?"

Donatra looked at Suran, whose teeth were still clenched. "Commander, a moment."

She rose from the table and walked into the vast recesses of the empty hall as Suran followed. In a low voice, Donatra asked, "Are you truly prepared to have your hands drenched in blood? He'll show them no mercy. And his sins will mark us and our children for generations. Is that what it means to be a Romulan now?"

Suran gazed at her, but he said nothing. So Donatra went on, "I think you should consider that question, or else you may have a lifetime to think about it in the dilithium mines."

She turned and stalked away.

In the captain's ready room, just off the bridge, Dr. Crusher sat down with Captain Picard and Commander Riker. There was no doubt that Shinzon had ulterior motives, and the captain had to know how serious they were.

"The more I studied his DNA, the more confusing it got," she began. "Finally I could only come to one conclusion: Shinzon was created with temporal RNA sequencing. He was designed so that at a certain point his aging process could be accelerated to reach your age more quickly so he could replace you."

"But the Romulans abandoned the plan," said Picard.

"As a result, the temporal sequencing was never activated," said Crusher. "Remember, he was supposed to replace you at nearly your current age. He was *engineered* to skip thirty years of life. But since the RNA sequencing was never activated, his cellular structure has started to break down." She hesitated then said bluntly: "He's dying."

"Dying?" asked Picard in amazement.

Riker nodded as if it made perfect sense. "He wasn't designed to live a complete, human life span."

"Can anything be done for him?" asked the captain with fatherly concern.

Beverly shook her head. "Not without a complete myelodysplastic infusion from the only donor with compatible DNA. But that would mean draining all your blood."

That machine in the brig. After a moment, the captain asked, "How long does he have?"

"I can't be sure," answered the doctor, "but the rate of decay seems to be accelerating."

Jean-Luc frowned as he reached the logical conclusion. "Then he'll come for me."

CHAPTER 7

In his quarters, Data studied the B-4 android, who stood perfectly still, his eyes more blank and lifeless than usual. He had been deactivated, but Data had to talk to his brother. So he opened the panel at the back of his neck and inserted a small instrument. Data adjusted the positronic relay slightly, and the B-4 cocked his head and looked directly at him.

"Brother," said the B-4, "I cannot move."

Data nodded. "No, I have only activated your cognitive and communication subroutines."

"Why?" asked B-4, sounding like a puzzled child who'd been told he couldn't eat a cookie.

"Because you are dangerous," explained Data.

"Why?"

"You have been programmed to gather information that can be used against this ship," answered Data.

The B-4 cocked his head. "I do not understand."

"I know," said the Starfleet officer. "Do you know anything about Shinzon's plans against the Federation?"

"No," answered the B-4.

Data went on. "Do you have any knowledge of the tactical abilities of his ship?"

"No. Can I move now?" requested the B-4.

"No." Data took his tool and began another adjustment inside the B-4's circuitry.

"What are you doing?"

The B-4 sounded so trusting that answering him was difficult. "I must deactivate you," answered Data.

"For how long?"

"Indefinitely," responded Data.

After a moment, the B-4 asked, "How long is that?"

Data gazed into the trusting eyes of his nearly identical twin. "A long time, brother," he answered.

With another flick of his wrist, the B-4's eyes lost the spark of life, and his system functions ceased. He stood motionless, staring into Data's somber eyes as if he were still alive.

Captain Picard sat down at the conference table in the observation lounge, facing his senior staff. La Forge had promised them a briefing on the source of the Thalaron radiation from the *Scimitar*. This might give them a clue as to Shinzon's ultimate intentions.

The chief engineer looked at his comrades and said, "It's called a cascading biogenic pulse. The unique properties of thalaron radiation allow the energy beam to expand almost without limits. Depending on the radiant intensity, it could encompass a ship. Or a planet."

The captain scowled. "He would only have built a weapon of that scope for one reason: He's going after Earth."

In alarm, Deanna Troi turned to him. "How can you be certain?"

Picard shrugged. "I know how he thinks."

"Destroy humanity, and the Federation is crippled," muttered Riker.

"And the Romulans invade," said the captain.

Riker looked back to La Forge at the head of the table. "There's no way to penetrate his cloak?"

"No, sir," answered the engineer.

The first officer slammed his fist into his palm. "He could pass within ten meters of every ship in Starfleet, and they'd never know."

A moment of grim silence followed, and Dr. Crusher finally spoke to Picard. "But we do have one advantage: He needs your blood to live. He might come after you first."

"I'm counting on it," vowed Picard. "We've been ordered to head to sector one-zero-four-five. Starfleet is diverting the fleet to meet us there."

"Strength in numbers?" asked Riker.

"We can only hope so," said Picard gravely. "He can't be allowed to use that weapon. All other concerns are secondary. Do you understand me?"

Commander Riker understood perfectly, because they both knew the *Enterprise* was expendable. Earth was not.

"Yes, sir," answered the first officer.

Captain Picard stood and pressed the comm panel. A moment later his voice echoed throughout the ship:

"All hands . . . battle stations."

The captain spent the next two hours touring the ship, watching preparations he hadn't seen since the Dominion War. Regular and backup crews were stationed in the weapons bays, shuttlebays, bridge, engineering, and auxiliary stations, in case any became compromised. Squadrons of security officers were armed with phasers in case they were boarded. Two of them became the captain's bodyguards.

In engineering, La Forge and his team set up emergency force-fields around the warp core and double-checked shield harmonics. Riker held one briefing after another with the officers from various departments, making sure everyone knew they were fighting to the death. On the bridge, Data never left his science station, where he entered all the information he had learned while on Shinzon's ship. Then he analyzed it from every possible angle.

As he prowled the corridors, Picard often stopped to talk to the younger officers—the ones who hadn't seen much action. He bucked them up and asked about their families on Earth or wherever. There was a point to this, because he wanted them to know exactly what was at stake. He gave each one a firm pat on the shoulder before he went on to the next station.

Stopping in his ready room, he made a brief entry in his log: "We're heading toward Federation space at maximum warp. The crew has responded with the dedication I've come to expect of them. And like a thousand other commanders on a thousand other battlefields throughout history, I wait for the dawn."

Minutes later he stopped by sickbay, where preparations were also in full swing. Dr. Crusher and her staff prepared the antigravity gurneys, hyposprays, tricorders, splints, and stasis chambers they would need to treat the wounded. Even here, there were armed security officers, and Beverly herself wore a hand phaser on her belt.

Picard stepped to her side and said, "'To seek out new life and new civilizations . . .' Zefram Cochrane's own words. When Charles Darwin set out on the *H.M.S. Beagle* on his journey into the unknown, he sailed without a single musket."

"That was another time," replied Beverly.

The captain scowled. "How far we've come. . . . Let me know if you need anything."

He started for the door, and the doctor stopped him. "Jean-Luc," she said gently, "he is not you."

He gazed at her, knowing that she was only partly right.

On the dark bridge of the *Scimitar,* Praetor Shinzon squirmed under the healing touch of his Viceroy. He felt ill, anxious, and wracked with minor pains, even as the lines on his face grew worse. The Viceroy was an expert at concealing his emotions, but Shinzon could see the toll his treatment was taking. He could also see the worry in the old Reman's pale eyes.

"How long?" asked the Praetor.

The Viceroy removed his hand from Shinzon's chest and sighed. "A matter of hours. You must begin the procedure now."

The young man slammed his fist on the arm of his

command chair, and the Viceroy backed away. After taking a deep breath, Shinzon regained his calm and sunk back in his chair. "How long until we reach the Rift?" he asked.

The Viceroy checked his console and replied, "Seven minutes."

Shinzon nodded, satisfied that they still had time. He looked at the overhead viewscreen, where the *Enterprise* was clearly visible just below them. He felt as if he could reach out and touch the famous starship, and the poor fools had no idea he was so close. He changed the view so that he could see the region of space known as the Bassen Rift—a colorful stew of electromagnetic distortion, crackling with energy.

It would be the graveyard of the starship *Enterprise*.

Making his rounds, Picard entered engineering during the late shift, where he found Data hard at work on a cartographic hologram. The warp core hummed in the background, surrounded by security officers and portable shield arrays.

The captain walked up to the immense star chart and said, "Show me our current position."

Data made an adjustment, and a tiny blip began to blink just outside the Bassen Rift. "How long until we reach the fleet?" asked the captain.

"At our current velocity," said Data, "we will arrive at

sector one-zero-four-five in approximately forty minutes."
He brought up the sector on the cartographic display.

Picard gazed at the images and said softly, " 'For now we see but through a glass darkly—' "

"Sir?" asked Data.

The captain replied, "He said he's a mirror."

"Of you?" asked the android.

"Yes."

Data cocked his head. "I do not agree. Although you share the same genetic structure, the events of your life have created a unique individual."

The captain looked closely at his old comrade. "And if I had lived his life? Is it possible I would have rejected my humanity?"

"No, sir, it is not possible," answered Data with certainty. "The B-4 is physically identical to me, although his neural pathways are not as advanced. But even if they were, he would not be me."

"How can you be sure?" asked Picard urgently.

"I aspire, sir," answered the android, "to be better than I am. The B-4 does not. Nor does Shinzon."

Picard considered that for a moment, taking some comfort from his words. "We'll never know what Shinzon might have been had he stood where I did as a child . . . and looked up at the stars."

*Had the Romulans turned the abandoned child over to
the Federation,* thought Picard, *it might have been different
for Shinzon.* But the Romulans' web of secrecy often
ensnared themselves as well as others.

"We are passing through the Bassen Rift," said Data,
highlighting that part of the chart. It shimmered oddly.
"The projection will return when we have cleared it."

"It's interfering with our uplink from Starfleet cartography?" asked Picard.

The android nodded. "The Rift effects all long-range
communications."

A sense of alarm seized the captain, and he barked into
the comm panel, "Commander Riker, evasive maneuvers!"

But it was too late as the *Enterprise* was wracked by a
photon torpedo blast. Behind them the warp core pulsed
erratically.

The *Enterprise* dropped out of warp with a lurch and
went spinning into the crackling swirls of the Bassen Rift.
From above, disruptor beams slammed the vessel, sending
energy ripples all along its sleek hull.

On the bridge of the *Scimitar,* Shinzon smiled with satisfaction at the beating his ship was giving the Starfleet vessel. "Target weapons systems and shields," he ordered. "I
don't want the *Enterprise* destroyed."

His Reman warriors silently obeyed his orders, specifically targeting the *Enterprise* for another volley. Shinzon looked at the viewscreen and asked his elder, "Can you learn to see in the dark, Captain?"

Captain Picard dashed onto the bridge of the *Enterprise* to see his crew glued to their stations, even while the ship rocked from another attack. "Report!" he demanded.

"He's firing through his cloak," answered Riker. "We can't get a lock."

From his engineering station, La Forge added, "He disabled our warp drive with his first shot. We've only got impulse."

"Long-range communication is impossible as long as we're in the Rift," said Worf.

Picard turned to the big Klingon and said, "Worf, prepare a full phaser spread, zero elevation. All banks on my mark. Scan for shield impacts and stand by photon torpedoes."

"Aye, sir," answered Worf, working his console with a purpose.

"Fire," barked the captain.

The *Enterprise* fired everything she had simultaneously, and the Rift was ablaze with dueling energy beam. The *Scimitar*'s shape was momentarily illuminated as photon torpedoes raked its shields. The Reman vessel made evasive maneuvers and once again turned invisible.

"You're too slow, old man," said Shinzon on the bridge of the warbird. "Attack pattern Shinzon Theta," he ordered.

The *Enterprise* reeled under the continued assault, and the bridge crew studied their readouts somberly.

"We are losing dorsal shields," reported Data.

Picard ordered, "Full axis rotation to port! Fire all ventral phasers!"

On the viewscreen, they could see the shields on the *Scimitar*'s underbelly light up as the *Enterprise*'s phasers again raked her hull. But the attack was all too brief, and the warbird again retreated behind an invisible curtain. Their sensors were already useless, even more so in the electromagnetic interference of the Rift.

"Minimal damage to the *Scimitar*," reported Worf angrily.

Riker strode to the helm. "Defensive pattern Kirk Epsilon. Geordi, get those shields on-line."

Picard looked around the bridge and didn't see Deanna. He tapped his commbadge. "Counselor Troi, report to the bridge."

The first officer muttered, "Unless we can disable his

cloak, we're just going to be firing in the dark."

"Agreed," said the captain.

"Sir, we're being hailed," relayed Worf.

"On screen," said Picard grimly.

Praetor Shinzon appeared on the viewscreen, surrounded by his calm bridge crew. "Captain Picard," said the arrogant young man, "will you join me in your ready room?"

With a curt nod, Picard strode into the private office, where he was surprised to find Shinzon sitting at his desk. When the Praetor rose and passed through Picard's desk, he knew it was some sort of holographic projection.

"You can't trace my holographic emitters, Captain," said Shinzon. "So don't bother trying. And you can't contact Starfleet. It's just the two of us now, Jean-Luc, as it should be."

"Why are you here?" snapped Picard, unwilling to make small talk. If he were, he would ask about Shinzon's face, which now looked like a map of diseased veins.

"To accept your surrender," answered the Praetor. "I can clearly destroy you at any time. Lower your shields and allow me to transport you to my ship."

"And the *Enterprise*?" asked the captain.

Shinzon shrugged. "I have little interest in your quaint vessel, Captain. If the *Enterprise* will withdraw to a distance of one hundred light years, it will not be harmed."

"You know that's not possible," said the captain bluntly.

The young man's lips thinned. "I know. You'll all gladly die to save your homeworld."

Picard stared intensely at the younger version of himself. "Look at me, Shinzon. Your eyes, your hands, your heart, the blood pumping inside you—they're the same as mine! The raw material is the same! We have the same *potential.*"

"That's the past, Captain," answered Shinzon smugly.

"It can also be the future," insisted Picard. "Buried deep inside you—beneath the years of pain and anger—is something that has never been nurtured: the potential to make yourself into a better man. To make yourself more than you are. *That's* what it is to be human."

The Praetor looked at him with clenched jaw, but Picard refused to give up. "Yes . . . I know you. There was a time you looked at the stars . . . and dreamed of what might be."

"Long ago," answered the young man softly.

"Not so long."

The Praetor looked at him with pity. "Childish dreams, Captain . . . lost in the dilithium mines of Remus. I'm what you see now."

"I see more than that." Picard stepped toward his young

double and looked at him warmly. "I see what you could be."

Shinzon recoiled and backed away, but Picard pursued the image across his ready room. "The man who is Shinzon of Remus *and* Jean-Luc Picard won't exterminate the population of an entire planet! *He is better than that!*"

The young man shouted back, "*He is what his life has made him!*"

"And what will he do with that life?"

Shinzon peered at his elder, unsure what he meant. Picard went on, "If I were to beam to your ship—let you complete your medical procedure, give you a full life— what would you do with the time?"

The young man narrowed his eyes suspiciously, and Picard explained. "If I gave you my life, what would you do with it? Would you spend the years in a blaze of hatred as you do now?"

"I . . . don't know," admitted Shinzon.

"You once asked me about your past," said Picard. "Your history. Let me tell you about mine. When I was your age, I burned with ambition. I was very proud, and my pride often hurt people. I made every wrong choice a young man can, but one thing saved me: I had a father who believed in me, who took the time to teach me a better way. You have the same father."

From the sadness in the young man's eyes, Picard knew he had made a connection. "Let me tell you about our father—," he began.

Shinzon looked away as if he couldn't bear to hear such sentiments. "That's your life . . . not mine."

"Please—"

"It's too late," insisted Shinzon.

Picard shook his head. "Never! Never. You can still make a choice. . . . Make the right one now!"

"I can't fight what I am!" said the confused youth.

"You can!"

A look of triumph came over the Praetor's face. "I'll show you my true nature . . . *our* nature. And as Earth dies, remember that I'm forever Shinzon of Remus! And my voice will echo through time long after yours has faded to a dim memory."

With a flick of his hand, the holographic image faded to a few phantom sparkles. Picard's shoulders slumped, as if all his strength and hope had left him.

CHAPTER 8

Praetor Shinzon entered the bridge of the *Scimitar,* still angry about Picard's attempts to divert him from his destiny. The old man was soft and pious, the victim of an indulgent, degenerate society. Instead of learning the power of hatred, Jean-Luc had gazed dewy-eyed at the stars. Tilling the soil, making beverages—this couldn't be the blood which flowed through the veins of Shinzon. Picard had to be lying about their family, too.

The ruler sunk into his command chair and looked at the Viceroy. "Disable their weapons!"

Before his order could be carried out, the Reman tactical officer said, "Two ships decloaking, sir." He paused to make sure, then added, "*Romulan!*"

Shinzon spun toward the viewscreen, where two

hawkish Romulan warbirds shimmered into view. Now the *Enterprise* was completely surrounded.

"Just when I thought this couldn't get any worse," grumbled Riker, staring at the trio of warbirds on the viewscreen.

Picard sat in his command chair feeling exhausted. He was glad that Deanna Troi was now at his side, looking calm in the face of the storm. If they had to die, it would be with the best of comrades.

"We're being hailed," reported Worf.

Picard rose to his feet, stiffened his spine, and motioned to the viewscreen. The striking figure of a female Romulan commander, bedecked in her ornate uniform with exaggerated shoulders, appeared before him. Captain Picard braced himself, expecting to hear more demands for surrender.

"Captain Picard," she began, "Commander Donatra of the warbird *Valdore*. Might we be of assistance?"

"Assistance?" asked Picard, puzzled.

The beautiful commander frowned. "The Empire considers this a matter of . . . internal security. We regret you've become involved."

He allowed himself a slight smile. "When this is over, I owe you a drink."

"Romulan ale, Captain," she replied. "Let's get to work. *Valdore* out."

The transmission ended, and the energized captain turned to Worf. "You heard the lady. Get to work."

"Aye, sir!" answered Worf with gusto. The Klingon pounded his board, and they began to fire phasers. Under what remained of their impulse power, the *Enterprise* charged into battle. A steady barrage from the two Romulan ships revealed the *Scimitar,* despite her cloak. Worf began to blast away with phasers at pointblank range.

Picard nodded with satisfaction, then said to Worf, "Coordinate our attack with the *Valdore*'s tactical officer. Triangulate fire on any shield impacts."

The *Scimitar* returned fire on the weakest of the three ships, and the bridge crew were knocked off their feet.

"Aft shields are down to forty percent," said Data.

Riker moved toward the helm and ordered, "Keep our bow to the *Scimitar.* Auxiliary power to forward shields."

For several moments it was chaos inside the churning Bassen Rift as deadly beams crisscrossed and the great ships jockeyed for position. The *Scimitar* broke off her attack on the *Enterprise* and began to concentrate all her firepower on one of the Romulan warbirds. Picard stepped toward the screen, concern on his face. If they had unleashed that barrage on the *Enterprise,* they'd be nothing but space dust by now.

Of course! Shinzon has to keep me alive.

Suddenly a massive array of disruptor banks on the bow of the *Scimitar* fired at once, cutting the Romulan warbird in half. It exploded with a blazing rupture of gas and debris that pummeled the *Enterprise*'s forward shields. The bridge rocked again, and the crew held on for dear life.

"Forward shields are down to ten percent," reported Data, which meant they couldn't survive another attack like that.

"Bring us about!" ordered Riker.

The *Enterprise* executed a graceful turn, unleashing their aft phasers on the *Scimitar*. The second Romulan ship pressed her attack, and the Reman vessel retreated. With excitement, Picard watched the *Valdore* chase the cloaked ship deeper into the swirling clouds of the Bassen Rift, firing on her tail.

On the bridge of the *Scimitar,* Shinzon waved his hand with disregard. "Let her pursue. Drop cloak on the aft port quadrant, and prepare for full emergency stop."

"What?" asked the Viceroy, startled.

"You heard me," said Shinzon with irritation. "Donatra will think we're damaged . . . losing our cloak."

As the Reman carried out his orders, Shinzon noted with satisfaction that the traitorous *Valdore* was closing on them, expecting an easy kill.

"She's almost on us," warned the Viceroy.

Shinzon held up his finger. "Not yet—"

He peered at the viewscreen, watching the *Valdore* gain on them, blasting their exposed stern. The aft shields appeared to be weakening.

"Praetor?" said the Viceroy urgently.

Shinzon nodded. "Full stop and fire!"

The *Scimitar* jerked to a sudden top, allowing the *Valdore* to sail past her. While the Romulan disruptors were blasting empty space, the *Scimitar* unleashed a volley of photon torpedoes that tore into the *Valdore*'s underbelly. The proud Romulan warbird careened out of control, energy pulses rippling along the length of her hull.

Shinzon nodded with satisfaction and said, "Restore the aft cloak and bring us about."

Captain Picard stared at the stark image on the *Enterprise* viewscreen, unable to believe what he saw. The bridge of the *Valdore* lay in ruins, sparks and fires burning everywhere. Bloody and wounded, Commander Donatra dragged her body off the deck to greet him.

"I'm afraid that drink will have to wait, Captain," she rasped.

He nodded gravely. "Do you have life support?"

"For the moment," she answered. "But we're dead in the water."

"Understood—"

The captain started to say more, but another volley slammed the *Enterprise,* knocking him off his feet. A chain of explosions ripped away chunks of the *Enterprise*'s hull, and debris from several decks spilled into space.

Data reported. "We have lost structural integrity on decks twelve through seventeen, sections four through ten."

"Emergency force-fields are holding," said La Forge.

Riker got on the comm channel. "Evacuate those decks and reroute field power to forward shields."

Picard looked grimly at the image of their gaping hull on the viewscreen. He was woefully short of options, and the best option he really disliked. But the captain knew that if he were dead, Shinzon's life might be mercifully short.

Deanna Troi touched his arm and gazed at him with intensity. "Captain, I might have a way to find them."

"Counselor?" he asked.

"The one thing he may have forgotten in the course of battle," she answered. "Me."

"Make it so."

Troi nodded and crossed the bridge to Worf's tactical station.

• · • · •

Praetor Shinzon studied the readouts on the arm of his command chair, wondering how best to destroy what remained of the *Enterprise*'s shields. Then he could transport Picard to the brig and destroy the Starfleet vessel at his leisure. This had to be done somewhat delicately, so as not to destroy the *Enterprise* too soon.

He turned to his Viceroy and said, "Prepare a lateral run—all starboard disruptors."

Before the Viceroy could reply, his eyes widened in alarm, and his whole body stiffened. "No!" he gasped.

"What is it?" demanded Shinzon.

"She is here," hissed the Reman.

Deanna Troi staggered on her feet and gripped Worf's tactical station for support. Her left hand continued to move over his targeting display, searching for their foe. She clutched her forehead in pain. "He's resisting me."

The Klingon could do nothing, and neither could her shipmates. This job was up to her. Somehow Troi maintained her concentration, although her head throbbed with the effort. Her legs felt weak, and her breath came in gasps. Still she continued to probe for the feral Reman, the same way he had looked for her.

"Remember me?" she asked, certain he could see her face in his mind. She had found him.

Deanna's eyes popped open, and she set the coordinates on Worf's board. "Now!" she shouted.

With a grunt, the big Klingon unleashed a full volley of photon torpedoes, concentrated in a tight circle. Everyone turned to the viewscreen to see the torpedoes find their mark, blasting the bridge of the *Scimitar*. A massive pulse rippled along the hull, causing the entire ship to decloak.

Picard jumped to his feet. "Fire at will!"

The *Enterprise* continued to attack with everything she had, but the big warbird banked swiftly and went into evasive maneuvers. Then the *Scimitar* returned fire from her aft disruptors, and more chunks of the *Enterprise*'s hull were blasted away. Lights flickered on the bridge, and burnt circuits sparked their last. *If only our shields weren't already so weak,* thought Picard, *we could make a real stand now.*

"Captain," said Data, "we have lost ventral shielding on deck twenty-nine."

"Divert power and compensate," ordered Picard.

An alarm klaxon sounded on the bridge, and Worf shouted, "Intruder alert!"

Riker dashed toward the turbolift, motioning to Worf. "Let's go!"

As they headed into the turbolift, Worf barked into his commbadge, "Security detail to deck twenty-nine."

As the doors closed behind them, Worf turned to his

comrade and said, "The Romulans . . . fought with honor."

Riker nodded somberly. "They did, Mister Worf."

A moment later the two comrades were moving down the corridor, leading a squadron of Starfleet security officers. Commander Riker fell back to check his tricorder for Reman life signs, when disruptor fire streaked down the corridor. Worf and his men had charged right into the Reman intruders, who seemed to number about a dozen. He thought he saw the Viceroy among them—the creature who had violated his wife's mind.

Worf snarled and waded into the smoke and explosions, laying down a stream of phaser fire. His men were right at his side, and a few of them fell to the disruptor beams. Riker got a bead on the Viceroy with his tricorder, and he was on the move. Braving disruptor fire, Riker rounded the corner in time to see the tall Reman open a Jefferies Tube and slip into the vertical passageway.

"Worf!" called Riker, giving his comrade a hand signal.

At once the Klingon rolled into the corridor, spraying phaser beams at the Remans. The enemy fell back, and Riker used his cover fire to dash to the Jefferies Tube. He ducked into the shaft which ran between decks and descended into the darkness.

• • • • •

On the bridge, Captain Picard still felt helpless as he watched the *Scimitar* fire upon them at will. The crew was jolted as an explosion ripped the saucer section and the bridge. Their helm officer flew out of his seat into a gaping hole, and everyone clung to their seats until the emergency force-field flickered into place. Deanna Troi raced to take the officer's place at the helm.

The viewscreen was gone, but Picard could see the *Scimitar* through the hole in his bridge. The predatory ship banked around for another attack, then it began to shimmer. Parts of it disappeared, while other areas flickered.

"He's getting his cloak back," warned La Forge.

"We have exhausted our compliment of photon torpedoes," said Data. "Phaser banks are down to four percent."

Picard scowled. "What if we target all phasers in a concentrated attack?"

The android shook his head. "The *Scimitar*'s shields are still at seventy percent. It would make no difference, sir."

The captain took a troubled breath, and Deanna Troi said, "They're stopping."

He turned to look through the hole in the hull. The *Scimitar* advanced slowly, more parts of its sleek hull vanishing.

"What's he doing?" asked La Forge.

Picard's jaw tightened. "He wants to look me in the eye."

Below decks, Riker stalked the Viceroy through a labyrinthine series of access tunnels. Flickering half-light and red emergency strobes of the crippled ship made visibility poor, but Riker knew these cramped passageways. However, the Viceroy was also in his element, accustomed as he was to little light.

Riker felt eyes upon him and crouched down, phaser ready. He peered into the darkness ahead and behind him but could see nothing, until he lifted his eyes upward. . . .

The Viceroy was hanging like a bat from the conduits in the ceiling, and he dropped down, knife slashing. Riker intercepted his knife hand, but he was knocked off his feet by the Reman's weight. Both of them crashed to the deck, where they rolled in life-and-death combat.

On the bridge, Captain Picard grimly watched the *Scimitar* maneuver into position only a few hundred meters away. Its great prow almost filled the gaping hole at the front of the bridge.

The glimmer of an idea shown on the captain's face. "We've got him." He sat in his command chair and began entering instructions to his crew.

"Sir?" asked La Forge puzzledly.

Picard answered, "He thinks he knows exactly what I'm going to do."

"We are being hailed," said Data.

"Deanna, stand by," ordered Picard. He motioned to Data. "Open a channel."

"I hope you're still alive, Jean-Luc," said Shinzon's arrogant voice.

"I am," answered Picard, still working his console.

"Don't you think it's time to surrender?" asked the Praetor. "Why should the rest of your crew have to die?"

Picard entered another command code, and Deanna looked back at him and nodded. He realized he needed more time, so he said, "Shinzon, I never told you about my first Academy evaluation, did I? I received very high marks for my studies. But I was found lacking in certain other areas. Personality traits, you might say. In particular I was thought to be extremely . . . overconfident."

He heard a sigh. "Captain, as much as I enjoy listening to you talk—"

Picard motioned to Data to cut the transmission, and Shinzon's voice stopped.

"Geordi," said the captain, "put *all power* to the engines. Take it from life support if you have to—everything you can give me."

"Aye, sir."

He looked toward the helm. "Deanna, on my mark."

"Ready, sir," she answered.

Picard leaned forward in his chair and raised his hand. "All hands, brace for impact! Engage!"

The starship *Enterprise* bolted forward in a final burst of speed—ramming speed. Picard could see the *Scimitar* make a desperate turn to port, but it was too late. With a shudder and an awful grinding noise, the Starfleet vessel plowed into the bow of the Reman warbird.

The collision sent everyone on both ships reeling. Picard staggered to his feet in time to see the saucer section ripping a hole in the *Scimitar*'s shuttlebay. Several of the small *Scorpion* shuttlecraft went flying off into space. When they finally came to rest, the two great ships were locked together by twisted metal, slowly rotating in space.

With thrusters blazing, the *Scimitar* jerked into reverse, trying to pull away from the *Enterprise.* Both ships groaned and shuddered, but they were joined by tons of wreckage. With a deafening shriek, the *Scimitar* finally pulled away a few meters.

In the bowels of the *Enterprise,* Riker and the Viceroy crashed from one bulkhead to another. Both their weapons were gone, and they had nothing but their bare hands. With

each violent wrenching of the ships, they staggered on their
feet, but they never stopped fighting. They wrestled and
punched each other like two behemoths in a fight to the death.

Gasping for breath, Riker spotted the access panel for
the power relays. As he grappled with the Reman, he
kicked off the access plate, and bright lights strobed from
the open panel. He dragged the Viceroy into the pulsing
light, and the blinded Reman threw up his hands. Riker
plowed into him with a beefy shoulder and drove him back
into an open Jefferies Tube. Gripping each other, they tum-
bled down the long vertical shaft.

As he fell, Riker grabbed a rung of the ladder and
slammed against the wall. The Viceroy struggled to hang
on, digging his talons into Riker's uniform. The Reman
still couldn't see well, and Riker pounded his face with all
his might. "Don't worry—Hell is dark!" shouted the
human.

With his last ounce of strength, Riker pried the
Reman's talon from his flesh and pushed him off. Grasping
nothing but air, the Viceroy fell into the darkness. His
shrieks echoed upward until an awful thud sounded from
the bottom of the shaft.

Wearily, the first officer dragged himself to the deck
and climbed out. From the way the ship was groaning, he
knew they weren't out of trouble.

CHAPTER 9

On the bridge, Captain Picard hung on to his command chair as the ship rocked back and forth. "Data!" he shouted. "I need you!"

The android was instantly at his side, and Picard yelled over the noise, "Computer! Auto-destruct sequence Omega. Zero time delay. Recognize voice pattern Jean-Luc Picard. Authorization alpha-alpha-three-zero-five."

The computer's synthetic voice replied, "Auto-destruct is off-line."

Picard grimaced and looked at Data, just as the *Enterprise* shuddered again. With a lurch, the *Scimitar* pulled free. Through the hole, they could see the damaged warbird slowly moving away under its own power.

Shinzon was going to escape.

• • • • •

With smoke still hanging in the air of the *Scimitar*'s bridge, Praetor Shinzon stared at the *Enterprise* on his viewscreen. The crazed captain had rammed him—such a pathetic, desperate maneuver. But it had proved one thing: Captain Picard was too dangerous and desperate to let him live.

Shinzon grunted and doubled over with sudden pain, because the sickness was getting worse. He could actually feel the veins throbbing on his face, and he could do nothing now that the Viceroy was off the ship. Shinzon realized that he was as doomed as his enemy, because the boarding party had clearly failed.

But the mission was still viable.

"Target disruptors," he said hoarsely. "Destroy them."

"Disruptors are off-line, sir," reported his tactical officer nervously.

With a grunt, Shinzon looked up. "Deploy the weapon. Kill everything on that ship. Then set a course for Earth."

The Reman gaped at him. "What about Picard?"

"Our greater goal is more important, brother," answered the Praetor. He glared at the image of the *Enterprise* on the screen. "Some ideals are worth dying for. Aren't they, Jean-Luc?"

The officer worked his board, and the bridge began to hum with ominous power. Dazzling energy beams coursed through the arches, conduits, and beams of the *Scimitar,* and Shinzon could feel the tiny hairs on his neck stand on end. The entire ship was charging itself for a monumental task.

Still fighting his illness, Shinzon stalked off the bridge into the antechamber which housed the thalaron activation matrix. A platform in the floor of the antechamber began to fold open, looking like the miniature weapon he had given Senator Tal'Aura. From the depths of this twisting, clicking mechanism rose a brilliant double-helix pattern of pulsing energy. A green beam moved slowly up the double helix, preparing to activate the thalaron matrix when it reached the top.

Now Captain Picard will truly know what it means to be assimilated.

Captain Picard and what was left of the bridge crew watched with alarm as the Reman vessel slowly began to unfold like some sort of intricate puzzle box. They had assumed the entire ship was a thalaron weapon, and now they knew they were right.

"How long until he can fire?" asked Picard.

La Forge checked his readout. "The targeting sequence should take about four minutes."

"But how can he?" asked Troi. "He'll kill you."

"This isn't about me anymore," answered Picard grimly.

However, he was determined to be the one who ended it.

The captain crossed to the weapons locker and pulled out a phaser rifle. "Prepare for a site-to-site transport," he told La Forge.

The engineer shook his head. "Captain, I don't know if the transporter—"

"That's an order, Commander," said Picard.

Data stepped forward. "Sir, allow me to go. You are needed here."

"This is something I have to do." He checked to make sure the phaser was set to full charge.

"Sir—" Data continued to protest, but Troi took his arm and looked at him.

"Let him go," she told the android.

Picard glanced at Data and said, "You have the bridge, Commander. Use all available power to move away from the *Scimitar*." He turned to the engineering station. "Now, Mister La Forge."

"Aye, sir," answered Geordi, not hiding his concern. Still he worked his console, and the captain disappeared in a swirling column of light.

A second later, sparks flew from the console. "That's it," said La Forge. "Transporters are down."

He exchanged worried glances with Deanna and Data. The captain was gone, and there seemed to be nothing any

STAR TREK

of them could do . . . but retreat at impulse power.

Data cocked his head thoughtfully. "Counselor Troi, please assume command. Geordi, if you will come with me." The android headed toward the turbolift, and La Forge could do little more than follow. But the engineer took his tricorder with him.

Moments later they stood on one of the decks which had been damaged in the fighting. In fact there was a large hole at the end of the corridor, where only an emergency force-field kept the void from sucking everything into space. Even here they could see the weirdly unfolding Reman spaceship powering up to destroy them.

Feeling uncomfortable so close to the breach in the hull, Geordi used his tricorder to activate another force-field around him and Data.

The android pointed to the Reman vessel. "What is our exact distance?"

La Forge checked his readings. "Four hundred and thirty-seven meters."

"Thank you." He assumed a runner's crouch, and Geordi looked at him with alarm. It was suddenly obvious what his friend intended to do.

"Thank you, Geordi," said Data, sounding as if he were grateful for their friendship of fifteen years and everything else in his life.

130

Unable to respond, the engineer tried not to think about what they were doing. Desperate times called for desperate measures. With his tricorder, he momentarily turned off the force-field around them, and Data took off running. Geordi turned back on his force-field and waited until Data was nearly on top of the hole in the hull, then he turned off the emergency force-field.

The android dove off his feet and went sailing out of the hole into the swirling space of the Bassen Rift. Aided by the decompression, he shot outward as if launched from a cannon. As soon as Data was clear, Geordi turned the force-field on near the hole and rushed over to watch his friend's progress.

He saw the android hurtling through space; Data looked as if he would miss the shifting alien craft. At the last second, he slammed into some cloaked part of the *Scimitar* and held on, and Geordi released his breath. Using his incredible strength, Data ripped open an access panel and managed to squirm into the alien vessel.

"You're welcome," said Geordi quietly.

"Praetor, there's an intruder on the ship," an officer reported to Shinzon.

The young man dismissed the Reman with a wave and looked back at the Thalaron matrix. Its double helix pulsed eerily in the darkness of the antechamber, and the green glow continued to climb toward the top.

The computer had begun the countdown: "Fifty-seven . . . fifty-six—"

Nodding with satisfaction, Shinzon turned and followed his underling back to the bridge of the *Scimitar*. The large viewscreen focused on the crippled *Enterprise,* which would cease to exist in less than a minute. He would enjoy the spectacle.

Suddenly the doors to the bridge blew inward with a terrific explosion that threw the Reman guards to the deck. Shinzon whirled around to see Captain Picard come storming in, his phaser rifle blazing. The Remans returned fire, but they had been caught off guard. Still, one of them managed to blast the rifle out of Picard's hands.

Thinking only of his precious thalaron weapon, Shinzon raced through the melee and into the antechamber. The computer's voice droned on. "Thirty-nine . . . thirty-eight—"

Shinzon could hear footsteps behind him, and he knew it was Picard. He drew his curved Reman knife and whirled around to meet him, but the captain caught his knife hand. The two of them grappled in the dimness of the antechamber, coming perilously close to the gleaming thalaron double helix.

With his fist, Picard knocked the knife out of Shinzon's

hand, and it skidded into the shadows. Shinzon looked about for another weapon and saw a disruptor which had been dropped by one of his guards. He dove for it just as Picard grabbed a long metal rod from the wreckage. Shinzon whirled around with his weapon as Picard thrust the rod into his stomach. Pain burned within him, but still he kept coming after Picard, trying to kill him . . . this symbol of his pain and suffering.

"Eighteen . . . seventeen—," the computer intoned.

Captain Picard struggled with all his might, but his suicidal foe collapsed upon him, pinning him against the bulkhead. The life was draining from Shinzon's eyes, yet he peered at him with triumph.

"I'm glad we're together now," wheezed Shinzon. "Our destiny is complete."

"Ten . . . nine—," the computer counted downward.

Picard struggled to move, but the dead weight was too heavy. A shadow flashed past him, and he looked up to see Data dash into the antechamber. The android popped open the panel on his wrist and removed a small silver disk. *The emergency transport unit,* thought Picard.

He grunted in protest when Data slapped the ETU onto his shoulder. A look of realization passed between them; only one of them was going to leave here, and it would be the captain.

"Seven . . . six—," droned the computer.

Picard reached for the ETU, but Data quickly activated it. "Good-bye," said the loyal officer.

As the room began to fade from view, the last thing Picard saw was Data drawing his phaser and aiming at the thalaron activation matrix. It was almost at its pinnacle. . . .

The captain slumped onto the deck of his own bridge, and he jumped up to see the *Scimitar* through the hole. The shifting starship suddenly exploded in a roaring blast, sending silvery shards spinning everywhere. Deanna, Geordi, and the rest of the bridge crew stared at him, still expecting another being to materialize beside him. But the captain was alone.

Geordi hung his head, and Deanna stared tearfully at the shimmering space debris. The realization sunk deeply into each of their hearts—Data was gone.

Picard surveyed his ruined bridge; it hardly looked as if they had won the battle. The emergency turbolift opened, and Commander Riker strode onto the bridge. He was bleeding and bruised and looked worse than any of them, but he was smiling.

At least Riker was happy until he saw the looks of grief on their faces. "Sir?" he asked.

When Picard couldn't answer, Deanna said softly, "Data—"

The first officer followed their eyes toward the glowing field of debris floating among the swirls of the rift. His big shoulders slumped, and he put his arm around his wife.

"Sir, we're being hailed," reported Geordi.

"On screen," answered the captain. Then he realized there was no screen anymore, so he said, "Open a channel."

An imperious voice said, "This is Commander Donatra of the *Valdore*. We're dispatching shuttles with medical personnel and supplies."

"Thank you, Commander," said the captain.

Donatra went on. "You've earned a friend in the Romulan Empire today, Captain. . . . I hope the first of many. I honor your loss. *Valdore* out."

With a sigh, the captain turned to La Forge. "Geordi, prepare the shuttlebay for arrivals. They don't know our procedures so just . . . open the doors."

"I'll take care of it, sir," answered the engineer without his usual enthusiasm.

"Number One, you have the bridge." Captain Picard headed to his ready room, feeling grief not only for Data and other crewmembers, but for Shinzon, the Romulans, and the Remans. In the end, ambition was perhaps the most deadly force in the galaxy.

CHAPTER 10

Several hours later Captain Picard felt he could entertain visitors in his quarters. He invited his senior staff—Riker, Troi, Crusher, La Forge, and Worf—with one missing. There was only silence among them, as no one could think of anything to say that would help.

He poured each of them a glass of Chateau Picard wine, then raised his glass. "To absent friends . . . to family." They drank their wine joylessly.

Riker smiled slightly as a remembrance crossed his mind. "The first time I met Data he was standing against a tree in the holodeck, whistling. I thought he was the funniest thing I'd ever seen. And no matter what he did, he just couldn't get that damn tune right."

The others smiled as they recalled their own memories

of Data. "And he couldn't tell a joke to save his life," said Geordi. "Do you remember when he created that holodeck program so he could practice stand-up comedy?"

That brought a round of laughter, but Picard grew somber. "Somebody needs to collect his belongings."

"I volunteer," said La Forge.

"As do I," seconded Worf.

Later that night, Worf and La Forge took storage units to Data's cabin and began collecting his most prized possessions. It was painful for Geordi to pick up Data's violin, his Sherlock Holmes hat and pipe, and his pictures of Dr. Soong. He let Worf take down Data's paintings and pack them in a crate, but he planned to take them to a gallery on Earth himself.

Fairly soon they had stripped the room down to regulation Starfleet issue, and they looked around for anything they missed. Suddenly Data's cat, Spot, leaped onto a table and meowed at them. With one more bound, he was in Worf's arms.

Worf held the feline, but he didn't look happy about it. "I am not a . . . cat person."

Geordi smiled. "I think you are now."

Spot settled into Worf's arms and began to purr. The Klingon looked at Geordi with alarm, like a warrior who had been captured by the enemy.

• • • • •

In the captain's quarters, Picard sat calmly at his desk, talking to his last guest of the evening. "I don't know if all this has made sense to you," he said, "but I wanted you to know what kind of man he was. In his quest to be more like us, he helped show us what it means to be human."

Across the desk from him, the reactivated B-4 android cocked his head. "My brother was not human."

"No, he wasn't," Picard admitted, "but his wonder and his curiosity about every facet of human life helped all of us see the best parts of ourselves. He embraced change because he always wanted to be more than he was."

"I do not understand," said the B-4 bluntly.

"Well, I hope someday you will," answered the captain.

Worf's voice broke in over the comm channel. "Captain, the *Hemingway* has arrived to tow us to spacedock."

"On my way," said the captain, rising from his chair. "Please notify Commander Riker."

On his way to the door, Picard glanced at the B-4. "We'll talk later?"

The android was staring blankly at the wall, and Picard looked away with disappointment. Then the B-4's voice rang out, "'Never saw the sun—'"

Picard stopped and turned around, realizing those were

words from the song Data had sung at Deanna and Will's wedding. The B-4 looked puzzled, unable to recall the next line of the verse.

"'Shining so bright,'" offered Picard.

"'Shining so bright,'" echoed the android.

Picard's face beamed with joy at these simple words from the android, who had just relived a moment from Data's life. Perhaps in time he would learn to appreciate the greatness of his brother's life.

Picard sighed and headed for the door, knowing they had a starship to put back together.

Three weeks later, the *Enterprise* was in spacedock, undergoing extensive repairs. The ship was still a disaster, but at least it was a bustling disaster. Captain Picard sat in his ready room, chatting with Beverly Crusher from her new office at Starfleet Medical. Beverly was gushing and looked happier than she had in years.

"You can't imagine them, Jean-Luc," she said joyfully. "They're kids! All with advance degrees in xenobiology and out to conquer every disease in the quadrant."

The captain smiled. "Reminds me of a young doctor I used to know."

Beverly went on. "They're running me ragged. Nothing but questions day and night. . . . I love it! Come to dinner, and I'll tell you all about it. There's a Bajoran band at the officers' mess."

"I'd love to, but I have so much work here." The captain motioned to a stack of reports, estimates, and procurement forms.

"Soon then," answered Beverly. "I'll save the last dance for you."

She ended the transmission just as Picard's door chimed. "Come," he replied.

Will Riker strode into the ready room, and Picard jumped to his feet. "Will!" he said warmly.

Riker smiled. "Permission to disembark, sir."

"Granted," said Picard with enthusiasm. "Where's the *Titan* off to?"

"The Neutral Zone," he answered confidently. "We'll be heading up the new task force. Apparently the Romulans are interested in talking."

"I couldn't think of a better man for the job," said Picard. He grew serious for a moment. "If I could offer you one piece of advice about your first command?"

"Anything."

Picard continued, "When your first officer insists that you can't go on away missions—"

"Ignore him," they both said at once.

"I intend to," said Riker with a grin. Now it was his

turn to grow serious. "Serving with you has been an honor."

"The honor was mine . . . Captain Riker," said Picard, coming to attention. They warmly shook hands.

Will nodded once more, turned on his heel, and headed onto the bridge. There he found technicians everywhere, with Geordi conducting them from his engineering station. Worf stood in the center of the bridge, glowering at a technician who was installing a new command chair. It did look rather ornate and technical, nothing like a seat for a proper Klingon warrior.

The gaping hole was still there, a reminder of how close they had all come to Data's fate.

The turbolift doors opened, and a young officer nervously strode onto the bridge. Trying to dodge around the work crews, he bumped into Riker.

At once the young man's face brightened. "Captain Riker?" he said. "Martin Madden—I'm the new First Officer."

"Commander," said Riker politely.

Madden looked around and lowered his voice. "I haven't, um, met the captain yet. I was hoping you could give me a little insight."

Riker nodded sagely. "Oh, well, the most important thing you need to know is that Captain Picard's not one of those by-the-book officers. He likes to keep things casual.

In fact, if you really want to get on his good side . . . call him Jean-Luc."

"Thank you, sir," said the new first officer gratefully.

Riker smiled but managed not to laugh out loud. He strode toward the turbolift, but he couldn't leave the bridge just yet. He had to stop and look around one last time at the place he had called home base for fifteen years. Geordi and Worf were both looking at him, bidding good-bye in their quiet way.

Will I ever find a poker game as good as this one? thought Riker sadly. Then he turned and entered the turbolift.

A moment later Captain Picard emerged from his ready room, and Commander Madden rushed toward him.

"Commander Martin Madden reporting for duty, sir," he said, snapping to attention.

Picard juggled some padds in order to shake his hand. "Welcome aboard, Commander. I hope your transfer didn't come as too much of a surprise."

"I was . . . honored," said the commander.

"I needed you immediately to oversee the refit," explained Picard. "As you can see, we have a lot to discuss. Shall we say dinner in my quarters at nineteen-hundred hours?"

"Very good . . . Jean-Luc," said Madden with a smile.

The way the captain narrowed his eyes at him, Madden knew that he'd been had. "Captain Riker was pulling my leg, wasn't he?"

Picard let him twist in the wind as he walked to the area where a young ensign was installing his new chair. Worf scowled at the sophisticated apparatus, but the ensign was eager to show it off to the captain.

"It's the Mark Seven, Captain," he said proudly. "State-of-the-art ergonomics . . . command interfaces with—"

Worf cut him off. "I told him you're comfortable with your old chair."

"Let's give it a try." Picard settled into his new command chair and looked around the busy bridge. The repair crews were all so young—even his first officer—it was like a new generation of fresh-faced kids to teach and nurture. He smiled at the youthful energy.

"Feels good," answered the captain.

Worf and Geordi looked at each other with surprise, but the young ensign beamed. "Try that button, sir," he suggested, pointing to the unfamiliar controls.

Picard pressed the button on the arm, and metal restraints flew from the cushions and wrapped around his waist and shoulders. *Safety belts,* thought Picard.

He smiled and said, "It's about time."

The captain pressed the same button, and the restraints retracted. With excitement, Picard motioned his new first officer to the second chair. "Commander, please sit down."

Madden did so, and Picard handed a padd to him. "We've received our first assignment. We're going to be exploring the Denab system. It should be exciting. It's a place . . . where no one has gone before."

The young officer beamed. It was clear that was exactly the kind of duty he sought aboard the legendary starship *Enterprise.*

JOHN VORNHOLT has had both writing and performing careers, ranging from being a stuntman in the movies to writing animated cartoons. After spending fifteen years as a freelance journalist, John turned to book publishing in 1989. Drawing upon the goodwill generated by an earlier nonfiction book he had written, John secured a contract to write *Masks,* number seven in the *Star Trek: The Next Generation* book series.

Masks was the first of the numbered *Next Generation* books to make the *New York Times* best-seller list and was reprinted three times in the first month. John has seen several of his *Star Trek* books make the *Times* best-seller list. Since then, he has written and sold more than fifty books for both adults and children.

Theatrical rights for his fantasy novel about Aesop, *The Fabulist,* have been sold to David Spencer and Stephen Witkin in New York. They're in the process of adapting it as a Broadway musical. In addition, *The Troll King* was just published by Simon & Schuster, and John is working on two sequels, which will be published in August and December of 2003.

John currently lives with his wife and two children in Tucson, Arizona. Please visit his Web site at: www.vornholt.net.

The most puzzling mysteries . . .
The cleverest crimes . . .
The most dynamic brother detectives!

THE HARDY BOYS®

FRANKLIN W. DIXON

Join Frank and Joe Hardy in up-to-date
adventures packed with action and suspense

Look for brand-new mysteries
wherever books are sold.

Available from Aladdin Paperbacks
Published by Simon & Schuster

2314-01

Test your detective skills with these spine-tingling Aladdin Mysteries!

The Star-Spangled Secret
By K. M. Kimball

Mystery at Kittiwake Bay
By Joyce Stengel

Scared Stiff
By Willo Davis Roberts

O'Dwyer & Grady
Starring in Acting Innocent
By Eileen Heyes

Ghosts in the Gallery
By Barbara Brooks Wallace

The York Trilogy By Phyllis Reynolds Naylor

Shadows on the Wall

Faces in the Water

Footprints at the Window

Want to add a little magic to your life?

Read all about

And discover what it's really like to be a witch!

Available from Simon Pulse
Published by Simon & Schuster

Looking for a great read?

MARGARET PETERSON HADDIX

Aladdin Paperbacks is the place to come for top-notch fantasy/science-fiction! How many of these have *you* read?

The Tripods, by John Christopher

- ❑ Boxed Set • 0-689-00852-X • $17.95 US / $27.96 Canadian

- ❑ The Tripods #1 *When the Tripods Came* • 0-02-042575-9 • $4.99 US / $6.99 Canadian

- ❑ The Tripods #2 *The White Mountains* • 0-02-042711-5 • $4.99 US / $6.99 Canadian

- ❑ The Tripods #3 *The City of Gold and Lead* • 0-02-042701-8 • $4.99 US / $6.99 Canadian

- ❑ The Tripods #4 *The Pool of Fire* • 0-02-042721-2 • $4.99 US / $6.99 Canadian

The Dark is Rising Sequence, by Susan Cooper

- ❑ Boxed Set • 0-02-042565-1 • $19.75 US / $29.50 Canadian

- ❑ *Over Sea, Under Stone* • 0-02-042785-9 • $4.99 US / $6.99 Canadian

- ❑ *The Dark Is Rising* • 0-689-71087-9 • $4.99 US / $6.99 Canadian

- ❑ *Greenwitch* • 0-689-71088-7 • $4.99 US / $6.99 Canadian

- ❑ *The Grey King* • 0-689-71089-5 • $4.99 US / $6.99 Canadian

- ❑ *Silver on the Tree* • 0-689-70467-4 • $4.99 US / $6.99 Canadian

The Dragon Chronicles, by Susan Fletcher

- ❑ *Dragon's Milk* • 0-689-71623-0 • $4.99 US / $6.99 Canadian

- ❑ *The Flight of the Dragon Kyn* • 0-689-81515-8 • $4.99 US / $6.99 Canadian

- ❑ *Sign of the Dove* • 0-689-82449-1 • $4.50 US / $6.50 Canadian

- ❑ *Virtual War*, by Gloria Skurzynski • 0-689-82425-4 • $4.50 US / $6.50 Canadian

- ❑ *Invitation to the Game*, by Monica Hughes • 0-671-86692-3 • $4.50 US / $6.50 Canadian

Aladdin Paperbacks
Simon & Schuster Children's Publishing
www.SimonSaysKids.com

PENDRAGON

Bobby Pendragon is a seemingly normal fourteen-year-old boy. He has a family, a home, and a possible new girlfriend. But something happens to Bobby that changes his life forever.

HE IS CHOSEN TO DETERMINE THE COURSE OF HUMAN EXISTENCE.

Pulled away from the comfort of his family and suburban home, Bobby is launched into the middle of an immense, inter-dimensional conflict involving racial tensions, threatened ecosystems, and more. It's a journey of danger and discovery for Bobby, and his success or failure will do nothing less than determine the fate of the world. . . .

PENDRAGON
A new series by D. J. MacHale
Book One: The Merchant of Death
Available now

Book Two: The Lost City of Faar
Book Three: The Never War
Coming soon

**From Aladdin Paperbacks
Published by Simon & Schuster**